"You didn't know your sister had triplets a little over a year ago?"

Jillian swung around to face him in a drift of sun-drenched-roses perfume. "And had been raising them on her own?"

Guilt flooded Cooper. Handling three infants on your own had to have been incredibly difficult. "No. I didn't know about any of it." He still could hardly believe it.

An awkward silence stretched out between them. "Apparently, she drove to your place first, but you weren't there."

Trying to absorb what had happened, as well as what was to come, Cooper asked, "Did Desiree say when she would be back?"

Jillian knotted her delicate hands in front of her, the frustration she'd felt earlier transferring to him. "Desiree wasn't specific, but I had the feeling it wouldn't be for a few days..."

A few days! "I can't take care of three babies!" Cooper blurted out.

Jillian's soft lips formed a disapproving frown. "Even if your sister needs you to do just that?" she asked quietly.

Dear Reader,

Families. Both a blessing and a burden. When we need them and they are there for us, helping and supporting, we are incredibly grateful. But when they don't agree with what we're trying to do...it is way too easy to become irritated.

No one knows this better than cowboy rancher Cooper Maitland. He loves his little sister dearly and was even her guardian for a time. But he's never agreed with any of her plans. And he really doesn't like it when she leaves her one-year-old triplets in his care—without even asking first! After all, what does he know about babies?

Luckily, his next-door neighbor Jillian Lockhart knows a lot about little ones. She is much more understanding about what his sister has done. Plus, she doesn't mind doing the neighborly thing and helping out with the kids.

Cooper is grateful for Jillian's help. He really comes to depend on her friendship. But when their attraction for each other flames wildly out of control, things start to get really complicated. Was it love drawing them together, or merely the false intimacy that comes from weathering any sort of trauma or hardship together?

Only time, and their hearts, will tell.

I hope you enjoy reading this book as much as I enjoyed writing it!

Best wishes,

Cathy Gillen Thacker

Their Texas Triplets

———

CATHY GILLEN THACKER

HARLEQUIN
SPECIAL
EDITION

If you purchased this book without a cover you should be aware
that this book is stolen property. It was reported as "unsold and
destroyed" to the publisher, and neither the author nor the
publisher has received any payment for this "stripped book."

HARLEQUIN®
SPECIAL EDITION™

Recycling programs
for this product may
not exist in your area.

ISBN-13: 978-1-335-40800-6

Their Texas Triplets

Copyright © 2021 by Cathy Gillen Thacker

All rights reserved. No part of this book may be used or reproduced in
any manner whatsoever without written permission except in the case of
brief quotations embodied in critical articles and reviews.

This is a work of fiction. Names, characters, places and incidents
are either the product of the author's imagination or are used fictitiously.
Any resemblance to actual persons, living or dead, businesses,
companies, events or locales is entirely coincidental.

This edition published by arrangement with Harlequin Books S.A.

For questions and comments about the quality of this book,
please contact us at CustomerService@Harlequin.com.

Harlequin Enterprises ULC
22 Adelaide St. West, 40th Floor
Toronto, Ontario M5H 4E3, Canada
www.Harlequin.com

Printed in U.S.A.

Cathy Gillen Thacker is a married mother of three. She and her husband reside in North Carolina. Her stories have made numerous appearances on bestseller lists, but her best reward is knowing one of her books made someone's day a little brighter. A popular Harlequin author, she loves telling passionate stories with happy endings and thinks nothing beats a good romance and a hot cup of tea! Visit her at cathygillenthacker.com for information on her books, recipes and a list of her favorite things.

Books by Cathy Gillen Thacker

Harlequin Special Edition

Lockharts Lost & Found

His Plan for the Quadruplets
Four Christmas Matchmakers
The Twin Proposal

Texas Legends: The McCabes

The Texas Cowboy's Quadruplets
His Baby Bargain
Their Inherited Triplets

Harlequin Western Romance

Texas Legends: The McCabes

The Texas Cowboy's Triplets
The Texas Cowboy's Baby Rescue

Visit the Author Profile page
at Harlequin.com for more titles.

Chapter One

"I wouldn't do that if I were you."

Cooper Maitland's low, teasing voice drifted through the sweet summer air.

Jillian Lockhart paused, one leg over the sill of her open bedroom window. Somehow, she wasn't surprised to see the ruggedly handsome cowboy loitering in the shadows beneath. Every time she turned around lately, the sexy young cowboy was there. Working. Observing. Doing whatever he could to get under her skin. And given how much he had shown up in her dreams lately, it didn't take much...

Every time she was near him she wondered what it would be like to be held in his arms. To allow him to steal a dance. Or maybe even a kiss...

Not that it was ever going to happen.

Know-it-alls like Cooper were *not* her type.

And besides, she had a boyfriend.

One who was way older and more sophisticated than the down-to-earth hired hand haunting her dreams.

Resting one foot on the roof of the porch, she reached inside to pull out a canvas duffel bag and toss it to the ground beneath. It landed in the grass with a low thud. And was followed by the backpack containing her ID, birth certificate and phone.

"I mean it, darlin'. This isn't smart. Not at all."

Ha! She slanted him a haughty glance, her pulse already racing. And she wasn't even near him yet. "Like you would know!"

"As a matter of fact, I do." He pushed the brim of his hat back to better survey her. "And I still wouldn't do that if I were you," he warned, even more critically.

She lifted a brow. "It's a good thing you aren't me, then," she called back softly.

And an even better thing that she didn't have time to stand there trading insults with him.

She tested the rope ladder she had strung from her bed to the ground. Satisfied it was still tight, she stepped all the way out onto the roof, closed the window as much as she could, and then climbed to the ground below.

Finished, Jillian turned back to him. He was still looking at her with those incredible sable brown eyes. Her heart racing, she moved closer, determined to show him she wasn't afraid to go toe-to-toe with him.

"Because if you were me, then you'd have a big, snooping family always sticking their nose into your business and telling you what to do!"

His grin widening, he surveyed her indignant expression. His intuitive eyes lassoed hers. "Or *not* do?"

She did her best to stifle a sigh while stubbornly holding her ground. She wished he didn't radiate such endless masculine energy or look so hot in a black T-shirt and jeans. "My personal life is none of their business!" she complained, wondering if he really was going to mess up her plans.

He shrugged. Sweeping off his Stetson and shoving a hand through the rumpled strands of his dark brown hair, he frowned and settled his hat squarely back on his head. "They care about you."

"Yeah, well…" She loved them, too. It didn't mean they were right about Chip Harcourt being too old for her. Age was irrelevant when it came to kismet. And they were definitely a couple who was meant to be together. They had both known that, from the very first time they had met. Beneath the shimmering canopy of a star-filled Texas night…

Jillian picked up her duffel crammed with everything she'd been able to take with her, and then her backpack. Both were ridiculously heavy.

For a moment she considered driving one of the cars out to meet her boyfriend. But knew she couldn't. The sound of a car engine at one in the morning on a weeknight would wake the dogs sleeping inside and then her parents.

And her plans to run away would be foiled.

With a sigh, she slung the backpack over one shoulder and picked up her duffel with her other hand. Then started down the half-mile lane to the highway where Chip would be waiting.

His steps as easy and virile as his appearance, Cooper fell into step beside her. "Want a hand with that?" he asked with choirboy innocence.

"No, thanks." Jillian puffed, waving an airy hand. Trying not to think what a dashing figure he cut, she turned her glance toward the horizon and said, "I'm sure you have some sort of ranch work to do right now." Her body temperature rising inexplicably, she dismissed him impertinently. "Lost cattle. Rustlers…to look for."

He chuckled and let his glance rove over her flirtatiously. "Actually, darlin', you're the only thing going on right now."

Trying not to notice how he towered over her—or how much she liked it—Jillian dropped her bag dramatically, glad for the excuse to put it down for a second, so she could give her already aching muscles a break. Then she put her hands on her hips and glared up at him, taking in his muscular six-foot-three-inch frame all the while. Between the full moon and starlit sky overhead, and the solar landscaping lights that framed either side of the long, elegant drive of the Circle L Ranch, they could see each other quite well.

"Don't tell me you're planning to follow me all the way to the highway."

He grinned and gestured noncommittally. Then came close enough she could smell the soap and manly fragrance of his skin. "Okay, then, I won't tell you."

Eyes narrowing, she huffed. "Listen, cowboy, this is none of your business."

He regarded her and said with breathtaking chivalry, "It's always a person's business when he sees a young lady in trouble."

Young lady! Was he serious?

He made her sound like she belonged in some silly Edwardian novel.

Heavens, this man was annoying!

Telling herself she did not need this handsome, sexy cowboy's protection, she turned on her heel and marched back to her things. Spine ramrod stiff, she hefted her bags onto her shoulders. "You're going to make me late."

He fell into step beside her, as she once again headed in the direction of the highway. His one long languid step matched every two of hers. Which for some reason only added to her fury. "Afraid Harcourt won't wait?" he prodded lazily.

Was she? It wasn't as if her secret beau had stood her up thus far. Yet, it did bother her how seldom they actually did see each other. Most of their communication was via the burner phone he had gifted her with. "Of course, he will!"

Cooper looked over at her curiously. "Then…?" he queried.

She was just nervous. Clearly Cooper wanted to know why.

Maybe the quickest way to get rid of him was to let him know she was already spoken for. Proudly, she lifted her gaze to his and announced, "It's not every day a girl elopes."

He took in her building excitement. The special care she had taken when doing her hair and make-up and picking out her clothes.

The appreciative gleam in his eyes made her feel the extra care had all been worth it. Even though, of course, she had done it for Chip, not him!

"So, in other words, this is your eighteenth birth-day present to yourself," Cooper drawled.

Wow, Jillian thought in pure astonishment, real-izing that the infuriating man knew not just exactly how old she was, but that it was her birthday, too! Her four brothers and three sisters could barely keep that straight! Of course, there were eight kids in the family… And her dad might have mentioned it in passing, since she knew her parents were planning a big party for her that coming weekend. A party she hoped would turn into a birthday slash elopement celebration. Once her marriage was a fait accompli…

"Or am I wrong about that?" Cooper persisted, studying her in mute disapproval.

Jillian had to put her bags down again. Hand to her chest, she paused to catch her breath. Cooper was still looking down at her, and when she gazed insolently back at him, she couldn't help but notice how completely protective he looked. Even if he was, like most everyone else in her life, hopelessly misguided. "No, you're not wrong about that," she answered finally. Aware that if she hadn't known better, she would have thought the goading cowboy didn't want her to get married and hence take herself "off the market," and leave Laramie County. "Although I would have said yes to Chip's proposal even if it weren't my birthday."

Cooper picked up her bags, hefting them as easily as half-filled paper grocery bags, and headed on down the lane. Leaving her to follow him at will.

He shot her a considering look over one shoulder. "He's that incredible a boyfriend?"

"Fiancé," Jillian corrected, rushing to catch up. And more than a little irked by the skepticism in his deep, male voice, replied. "And yes, he is."

Cooper leaned down so they were face-to-face. Mischief sparkled in his eyes. "I guess he's romantic then, too."

Jillian flushed self-consciously. "Very!" Not a day went by she didn't get a virtual bouquet, or playlist or a sweet love message from her boyfriend slash fiancé. He had even written her poetry! She couldn't imagine Cooper Maitland *ever* doing that.

"And an all-around good guy, too?" Cooper queried.

Defiantly, she ignored the niggling doubt that popped up at times like now. "Yes!"

He nodded at her. "Do your parents like him?"

Something else she would have preferred not to reveal. "They haven't actually met him," she admitted, her heart thumping once again.

Looking at her thoughtfully, he let his tone drop a confidential notch. "Why not?"

Pretending his attempts to delay her so they could continue their argument were not bothering her in the least, Jillian flashed a confident smile. "Because they refused to even let me introduce him to the family!"

A sardonic grin tugged at the corners of his lips. "How come?"

She bristled. "They think Chip is too old for me."

"So they know you've been seeing him," he said soft and low.

Damn, Cooper's voice was like velvet. She could wrap herself in it. If she were ever around him like that, that was. Not that she planned to be...

Pushing away the crazy burst of physical attraction, she drew a calming breath and reminded herself that Chip Harcourt was the love of her life, not the aggravating cowboy in front of her with the sable brown eyes that saw far too much...

Aware Cooper was still waiting for her explanation, she admitted in exasperation, "They know I wanted to date him. And have ever since I met him at a concert out at Lake Laramie in June. But they wouldn't allow it because he was twenty-four."

Cooper rubbed his hand across his jaw. "Hmm," he rumbled with a maddeningly affable shrug. "Three years older than me. That is old!"

So Cooper was twenty-one.

She didn't know why she found that so intriguing. It wasn't like she was interested in him or anything…

Oblivious to the direction of her thoughts, Cooper stepped closer still. He gazed down at her, as if trying to understand. "That why you've been sneaking out to see him for the last six weeks?" he asked her gently. Compassion and a need to understand filled the night air between them. "'Cause it was forbidden love and all that?"

Hearing it put like that made her feel even more out of her depth. Stifling a groan of dismay, she lifted her chin. "How do you know I was sneaking out…?" All the while she found herself studying the frayed collar on his T-shirt. The way his sinewy chest and shoulders filled out the dark knit.

His husky chuckle filled the warm night air. "Well, the rope ladder coming down over the roof after midnight every Wednesday night is kind of hard to miss."

Gosh darn it. She had been *so* careful not getting caught by her family even once!

"Not if you weren't looking," she told him.

"True." His eyes twinkled. "But as the newest

hired hand, part of my job is to patrol the ranch at night. Keep an eye out for stray cattle, rustlers."

She knew there had been a problem lately. That over the course of the summer several ranches had lost some of their herd. Especially the newborn calves. She scowled at him, her heartbeat accelerating. "Well, your job isn't to spy on me!"

Eyes still locked with hers, he shrugged his broad shoulders. "They were collateral sightings, that's all. And frankly—" he made no effort to hide his boredom "—not very interesting at that. All the two of you did was sit in Casey's—"

"Chip's!" she corrected, knowing he had gotten the name wrong on purpose to get under her skin. Which he had!

"Okay... *Chip's* convertible and talk for about thirty minutes before you went back to the ranch house."

Her mouth fell open. She didn't know whether to feel resentful or horrified. Certainly, she was embarrassed. "You *watched* us the whole time?"

He poked the brim of his hat back. His dark brows constricted in concern. "Well, up till today you have been underage, and I wanted to make sure you were okay. That some guy wasn't taking advantage. 'Cause then I would have been duty bound to step in. You, being a minor and all. But—" he tilted his head to one side, looking as relieved as she suddenly felt "—it looked like he never did."

No, Chip Harcourt hadn't.

Precisely because she had been underage.

But now, as of thirty minutes ago, she wasn't! So... Doing her best to suppress her continued mortification, Jillian squared her shoulders and drew herself up to her full five feet nine inches. The fact she was starting to have second thoughts about what she was doing was pre-elopement jitters, that was all.

She swallowed hard around the knot of anxiety in her throat. "Well, you needn't worry. Before anything like that happens, Chip Harcourt plans to marry me and make it all legal." Then she wouldn't have to hide. And she wouldn't have to lie. And she wouldn't have to feel so darn guilty all the time.

Cooper continued watching her curiously. "And then what?" he asked, his gaze sifting over her, taking in her burning cheeks and trembling lips.

Harsh experience had shown Cooper Maitland that no good could ever come of rescuing a damsel in distress. So it should have been easy to ignore sassy, headstrong Jillian Lockhart. It wasn't.

Part of it was the fact she was so strikingly beautiful. Her long-lashed sea-blue eyes were incredibly captivating, dominating the elegant features of her oval face, with its slightly upturned nose, prominent cheekbones and lush lips.

The rest was that she was so extremely determined to go down a path that could easily ruin the rest of her life.

Call him foolish. And maybe he was for putting

in jeopardy the job he had worked so hard to get. But he didn't want to see her hurt.

Not that he could fully prevent that now.

Because the situation was too far gone for that.

His body hardening, he let his gaze sift over her lithe and feminine frame. And once again, he tried to urge her to use her common sense. "What happens after you have a ring on your finger?" he asked, his fingers itching to explore the thick, silky mane of honey-blond hair cascading over her slender shoulders and down her back.

Jillian blushed.

For a second, he thought she wasn't going to answer. Whether because she didn't know or simply hadn't thought that far ahead, he did not know.

Curious, he prompted, "Your dad said you were leaving for Texas A&M in two weeks to study botany." He took in her white denim skirt, lacey blouse and peacock blue boots. "Is that still the plan?" He kept his gaze locked with hers. "Or are you giving up college for Chip Harcourt?"

For the first time, sorrow came and went in her expression. With a frown, she admitted, "I'm going to have to, temporarily anyway. Chip travels for work. So if I want to be with him, and I do, I'll have to go with him."

Cooper could only imagine how much fun that would be for a free-spirited, personally ambitious young woman like her. "And live in motels?" He stepped closer, invading her personal space.

Her spine stiffened. "I'm sure we will get an apartment somewhere."

Given what he knew about her "fiancé," he doubted that.

"I'll get my education eventually," Jillian promised.

But not wanting to argue with her, he merely nodded.

Resentment glittering in her pretty eyes, she picked up her backpack and slung it over her shoulder. "You don't believe me?"

He reached for her duffel bag and fell into stride beside her. "I believe your intentions are good."

In lockstep, they headed for the highway, now visible in the distance.

She tossed her head of silky blond hair. "But?"

Wishing he didn't desire her the way he had never desired anyone else, he told her what he had learned. The hard way. "Life…has a way of getting in the way of goals. Especially when you marry way too young. For all the wrong reasons."

She stormed on ahead. "Love isn't a wrong reason!"

Cooper hated the fact she had been duped. Her innocent heart all but taken by such an unscrupulous shyster. He moved to catch up. "Sure you know what love is?"

She narrowed her glance. "Of course."

Her self-conscious flush and evasive eyes said otherwise. "As opposed to passion," he continued, drinking in her bare, suntanned legs and the alluring rose fragrance of her perfume.

"I told you." She wrinkled her nose. "We're waiting."

It did not escape his attention that the first two buttons on her blouse were undone, revealing a triangle of creamy, soft skin above her breasts. "Surely he's kissed you so well he made your toes curl and your whole body tingle?" If Jillian had been Cooper's girlfriend, he sure as hell would have.

Not that he was going there.

He wasn't that foolish!

Protecting her from the jackass was going to have to be enough.

The look on her face said *No.*

Filling him with relief.

"I am sure it will happen," she insisted stubbornly. "Probably tonight."

Cooper was, too.

Trouble was, he didn't want it to happen. Any more than her folks did.

Her steps slowed as the empty highway came into sight. The lights that framed the archway into the ranch shone down upon them.

Still, no Chip Harcourt. No sign of his snazzy convertible. They set down her belongings. She pulled out her burner phone, looked at it.

Hoping the guy hadn't gotten wind of what was about to happen, Cooper asked her casually, "Any messages?"

She shook her head. "He'll be here." She slid her

phone back in her pocket, then ran her hand through her hair. Looking both aggravated and exasperated. "You don't have to wait."

Actually, Cooper thought wryly, he kind of did.

Headlights appeared in the distance. Seeing it was a convertible, Jillian breathed a big sigh of relief. "Okay. Now you really have to leave."

"How come?" Cooper said, stalling. "You think he'll be...jealous?"

She swung back to face him.

Their gazes locked. Something changed in her eyes, a flicker of uncertainty glimmering in their beautiful sea-blue depths. His pulse amped up as she drew another quick breath. "No. Of course not." She bit her lip, looking increasingly young and vulnerable. She cocked her head to one side. "Why would he be?"

Maybe because of the potent physical attraction shimmering between them. Attraction that had been there since the first moment they had laid eyes on each other.

And the fact that he sensed she secretly dreamed about kissing him every bit as often as he fantasized about kissing her...

Chip Harcourt's car neared. Slowed.

For a moment it looked as if he might just keep on driving. Until he saw who was standing next to Jillian, that was.

The unscrupulous jerk smiled and turned his car

into the drive. Then stopped, cut the engine. Got out. He strolled forward in a suit and tie.

He had a bouquet of white roses in hand. "What's going on?" he asked Jillian cautiously.

"Nothing." She tossed her backpack into the rear seat, then went back for her duffel. "Cooper was just seeing us off." She smiled, giving him a look that said he should exit. *Now.*

Cooper ignored her cue.

She sent him a withering glare only he could see. "Wishing us well," Jillian continued.

"Hmm." Chip studied Cooper. With a suspicious frown, he took the duffel from Jillian and put it in the back seat of his car beside her backpack. Handed her the bouquet.

And then everything happened very fast. Sheriff's vehicles approached from both directions, lights blazing, sirens wailing. And just as swiftly, blocked the ranch entrance.

Robert and Carol Lockhart got out of one of the squad cars. They were joined by Laramie County deputies Dan McCabe and Rio Vasquez, and several others from nearby counties.

"Chip Harcourt," Dan McCabe said, "we have a warrant for your arrest."

"For *what*?" Jillian cried, tremendously upset.

Cooper grabbed her and held her back before she could rush to her secret fiancé's aid.

Rio brought over a rap sheet that was pages long. "Bigamy, extortion, embezzlement, theft."

Her parents approached. "He's a con man."

"He is," Rio stated. "He targets young, impressionable women, talks them into eloping with him, and then offers to annul before the marriage is consummated, if the parents will pay him off. Which most do. He steals whatever he can from those who don't." Rio regarded Jillian sympathetically. "Right now he is romancing three underage girls simultaneously."

She gasped, still trembling. "I don't believe it!"

Reluctantly, Cooper handed her off to her parents, who surrounded her. "We're sorry, honey," Carol Lockhart said. "When we found out what was going on…"

"From Cooper…" Robert Lockhart added. "We went to law enforcement and had Chip Harcourt investigated."

Jillian broke away from her parents long enough to whirl on Cooper, looking stricken and completely betrayed. "So you knew all along!" she cried.

He lifted a placating hand, not sure what she expected him to say. "I didn't want to see you hurt."

Too late.

"So, you humiliated me instead!" Jillian countered bitterly. And it didn't take a genius to see that she was never going to forgive him.

Chapter Two

Ten years later...

Cooper put the last block of high-protein feed in the back of his pickup truck, while King watched intently from the front seat. He grinned at the handsome yellow Labrador retriever and shut the tailgate, then walked around to climb behind the wheel. "Ready to head home and tend some cattle, buddy?" he asked.

King wagged his tail enthusiastically.

Cooper reached for the ignition just as his cell phone went off, signaling an incoming text. He paused to check the screen. Barely able to believe what he saw.

The sender was Jillian Lockhart.

The message said: Family emergency at Rose-haven! You are needed here RIGHT AWAY!

"Family emergency?" Cooper muttered to himself. "What kind of crisis could be happening that would have Jillian Lockhart, a woman who hasn't had one word to say to me for the entire last decade, calling me?" Never mind *demanding* he go over to her ranch?

Unless, he thought, on a new wave of worry, the summons had something to do with her mom or dad. Whom he not only liked immensely, but owed for giving him his start in Laramie County and the ranching business.

Figuring the thing to do was get there first and ask questions later, he texted back, Be there in ten.

Luckily, there was little midmorning traffic that time of August, since school had started a few days before. He picked up speed as he left the Laramie, Texas, town limits, and headed west on the highway. Jillian's place was located next to her parents' spread. His was on the other side of hers.

Her dad's pickup truck was parked next to Jillian's red Tahoe.

Pulse accelerating, Cooper parked in the shade and rolled down the windows on his truck. Instructing his dog to *stay*, he jumped out and headed for the front steps of the refurbished Victorian farmhouse with the wraparound front porch. He had just reached the bell when the front door was flung open.

An adorable baby girl cuddled in her arms, a grim-looking Jillian faced off with him.

"What's going on?" he asked. Able to see her mother and her father in the open living area behind her, each with an identical baby girl in their arms.

Carol Lockhart handed the baby she held to Robert, then came forward to relieve Jillian of the one she was holding.

"Why don't you all talk outside?" Carol Lockhart suggested with a veteran social worker's ease.

Jillian agreed, her expression resentful. She stepped outside, her body as tense as it had been the night her engagement had ended. As for the rest of her? Well, she had been all reckless teen back then. But now, she was *all woman*. Confident. Capable. And excessively independent. Her body was as svelte as he recalled, her features just as elegant, her long-lashed eyes the same fantastic sea-blue.

She'd made some changes, of course. Her honey-blond hair was shorter. She wore it parted on the side; the casual waves fell to her shoulders and framed her face. Her attire was usually business casual, adjusted for the Texas weather. Today, however, she had on knee-length khaki shorts, a yellow camp shirt with the usual two buttons undone and sneakers.

Just squaring off with her, he felt his pulse race.

Determined to get to the bottom of this, whatever it was, he stepped closer and asked quietly, "Was this the family emergency?" *And if so, what in heck did it have to do with him?*

Her lower lip trembled and she offered a tight, officious smile. "Your sister couldn't find you, so she came here instead."

Sister. A familiar weight descended on his heart. "Desiree?" he croaked.

Jillian gaped at him. Apparently silently accusing him of Lord only knew what. Lips compressed, she surveyed him contemptuously. "So she was telling the truth? She *is* your sister?"

He tracked the color in her elegantly sculpted cheeks. "And not...?"

She folded her arms in front of her. "Your girlfriend!"

Cooper studied Jillian in stunned amazement. Could it be? *Was* she jealous? *Why?*

Not that he hadn't occasionally felt the same emotion when he'd seen her out to dinner with some random guy from time to time.

Not that that mattered, either. Whatever the relationships were, they never seemed to last.

But her romantic history was not pertinent. The crisis that had brought him here was.

"So was it your long-lost sister who was here?" Jillian demanded, impatiently tapping her foot.

He assessed the mixture of judgment and confusion in her eyes. "I don't know. I mean, I wasn't here and didn't see the woman. But if she said her name was Desiree..."

Or even *knew* Desiree.

Jillian reached into her back pocket and pulled out a folded piece of paper.

Scrawled across it, were the words *I don't know how else to say this. I need your help. And you owe me. So...please, Cooper. Do right by Sadie, Hallie and Tess.*

Jillian pulled out her phone. She showed him a photo of a dark-haired young woman in a Western shirt and jeans, standing on Jillian's front porch. His heart twisted at the sight of the only family he had left. Family he hadn't seen in a decade. "That's Desiree, all right," he admitted grimly.

Her sharp, assessing gaze met his. "The note?"

Cooper felt a flash of angst mixed with disappointment. He exhaled. "Her handwriting, too."

Her pretty face taut with concern, she sat down opposite him, crossing her sexy legs at the knee. She cupped her hands. "None of us knew you had any family."

Too restless to sit, he remained standing. "Desiree and I have been estranged since she ran off with a boyfriend at eighteen."

Her brow furrowed at his careful tone. "Which was...?"

His whole body tensed. "Right before I went to work for your dad at the Circle L Ranch."

She gave him a long, steady look laced with compassion. "And you haven't heard from her since?"

Embarrassed by his failure to make amends, Cooper raked a hand through his hair, admitting wearily,

"I tried contacting my sister. But Desiree never answered any of my calls or texts, and then she changed her phone number all together, so I took the hint and let her go. Figuring if she ever came to her senses, that she knew how to reach me." Because he hadn't changed his contact number.

Jillian sent him a surprised glance. "But she didn't."

He shook his head, the hurt he had stuffed deep down rising within him.

Jillian stood and began to pace the length of the porch. "You didn't know she'd been living in Dallas and had triplets a little over a year ago?" She swung around to face him in a drift of sun-drenched rose perfume. "And had been raising them on her own?"

Guilt flooding him, he bit down on a litany of swear words. Handling three babies on your own had to have been incredibly difficult. "No. I didn't know about any of it." He still could hardly believe it.

An awkward silence stretched out between them. Swallowing hard around the tight feeling in his throat, Cooper studied her, then said, "I don't understand why my sister came here, though."

Jillian slanted her head. "Apparently, she drove to your place first, but you weren't there."

"I was at the feed store in town, buying supplies."

Worried it might be getting too warm in the open cab, even with the windows open, Cooper walked over to let his dog out. He pulled out the travel water bowl behind the seat, filled it with bottled water and put it on the ground.

King lapped it up thirstily, then followed his owner back up the steps where Jillian remained, lounging against the white railing that rimmed the wraparound porch. Waiting and watching.

Still trying to absorb what had happened, as well as what was to come, Cooper asked, "Did Desiree say when she would be back?"

Jillian squared her shoulders, the action lifting the luscious curves of her breasts. "She'll let you know. But not for a while."

"A while," Cooper repeated.

She knotted her delicate hands in front of her, the frustration she'd exhibited earlier transferring to him. "Desiree wasn't specific, but I had the feeling it wouldn't be for a few days…"

A few days! "I can't take care of three babies!" Cooper blurted out.

Jillian's kissable lips formed a disapproving moue. "Even if your sister needs you to do just that?" she asked quietly.

For a long moment, Cooper looked torn, which was not something Jillian expected to see, and left her feeling like she was having another one of those crazy dreams that had plagued her for the last decade. Through college, and grad school and starting her own antique rose business.

The ones where he was rushing to save her from making another huge mistake. Where he always ended up taking her in his arms and lowering his head as if to kiss her. Which left her waking with a start…and the sobering realization that this would never happen.

Not when he still saw her as the foolish, head-strong, ridiculously impetuous kid she had once been.

Whereas Cooper had grown into his adulthood with ease, transforming from an ambitious cowboy for hire to a respected rancher with his own two-thousand-acre spread. And dozens of local women interested in him…

Not that he seemed to be thinking about anything but the problem at hand.

Cooper moved so she had no choice but to glance up at him. His demeanor was gruff. "How did Desiree seem to you?" he asked in a way that had her heart going out to him. He had always been both charming and strong. Unnervingly intuitive, too. Decisive. But now he looked truly at a loss. And if she had been in his place, she probably would have felt the same. It was definitely not fun when family made life difficult.

Still holding his gaze, Jillian searched for the proper adjective to describe the young woman who had breezed onto her front porch and rung the bell while her three babies waited patiently in their car seats. *"Determined,"* she said finally.

He gave her another double take, as if he, too, felt as if he were waking from a bizarre dream. "Determined to do what?" he countered, looking confused and upset. "Abandon her babies to a complete stranger?"

Knowing anger and/or resentment wouldn't help anything, Jillian waved off the irritable judgment.

She knew, better than most, how quickly events could spiral out of control if prompt action wasn't taken. She didn't want to see Cooper's three nieces' lives collapse, the way hers had after the explosion and fire that had taken her biological parents' lives. Or worse, see the family separated by well-meaning social services. Because trauma like that could be very hard to overcome.

"Only until such time that you could take them," she explained reasonably, relaying what his sister had said.

"Still..." He stood, brawny arms clamped in front of him, legs braced apart, radiating an impressive amount of testosterone and take-charge attitude.

Unable to help but note how good he looked in the way of tall, strong and sexy, Jillian said, "She didn't just leave them." *Even though she said she had been running late and that something very important was at stake. Something Desiree hadn't felt she could afford to lose out on...* "I *offered* to help, Cooper."

His gaze drifted over her, as if he were appraising one of the prime cattle he raised on his ranch. "Why?"

"Because I was worried—" *perhaps illogically* "—what might happen to the children if she couldn't find you and I didn't agree to step in temporarily."

Especially because she seemed to be holding back a whole lot more than she was willing to say.

His brow lifted. "So she was overwrought," he cut in, all harsh male judgment once again.

"More like desperate for help," Jillian corrected. "And since you are apparently the only family her girls have, aside from her, she needed *you* to help them all out. And, like she said in her note, for whatever reason, she thinks you owe her this."

Interestingly, Cooper did not dispute that.

"You still could have said no," he pointed out.

Now he was concerned that she'd been, what? *Too nice?* Jillian waved her hand in exasperation. "Maybe if I were someone else or lived somewhere else. But that's not the way things work in Laramie County, cowboy, and you know it. Here, neighbors help neighbors out."

He continued to look skeptical. His gaze roved her frame, dwelling on her feminine curves.

"You know, kind of like the way you helped me out when you stepped in to botch my elopement with Chip Harcourt?" she added sardonically before she could stop herself.

The moment the words were out, she regretted them. How had she managed to go ten years without once bringing up that humiliating catastrophe? Or even acknowledging his presence in any way? Yet here she was, speaking to him about the most intimate family matters.

His lips twisted. A look she could not decipher appeared in his eyes, then fled, just as matter-of-factly. Once again, she found herself wondering what it would feel like to be held in his arms. Kissed by him.

"Point made," he said dryly.

Jillian knew she'd always been reckless in the past, willing to swiftly follow the dictates of her heart. Apparently, given what had just happened, she was still quick to jump in now, when needed. And while she might be completely comfortable with that, Cooper was not. With good reason, given their years-long estrangement.

Swallowing around the sudden parched feeling in her throat, she continued explaining her unprecedented willingness to be involved with anything at all that concerned him.

"I didn't know what you—or any single guy faced with a similar situation—might say in that particular moment. But I had a feeling it wasn't what Desiree needed to hear. So—" she wet her lips "—I stepped in to help you both out."

"I'm guessing my sister was grateful." His voice was as masculine as his presence.

"Very."

Silence strung out between them.

His gaze sifting over her thoughtfully, he asked, "How did she get here?"

Jillian put aside the notion of what it might be like to interact with him like this all the time. "A man drove her."

As their eyes met, a new warmth spiraled through her. "Do you know who he was?"

Ignoring the sudden wobbliness of her knees, she shook her head. "He never got out of the SUV."

Cooper lifted a brow. "Not even to help bring the babies in?"

"No," Jillian admitted reluctantly. Now that she thought about it, that seemed a little strange, too.

He edged closer, inundating her with his soap and sun-warmed leather scent. "Do you think my sister is in danger?"

Jillian ignored the thrill their closeness engendered. Working to slow her racing pulse, she met his eyes and responded with an inner calm she couldn't begin to feel. "From her companion? No. I didn't get that vibe at all. It was more like…" She struggled to find the right word. "*Excitement.* The kind you get when you finally get your first taste of freedom or adventure after a long while without it."

The kind I get whenever I'm this physically close to you.

Cooper scrubbed a weary hand over his ruggedly handsome face. "So a new romance is behind all this?"

She gestured uncertainly. But figuring she owed him as much information as she could give him, even if it was purely speculation, she admitted, "Something seemed to be going on behind the scenes."

"Did she at least leave a phone number?"

She pulled out her phone, happy about that much. "I insisted on that." She texted it to Cooper.

"Thanks." He checked his screen, hit Call...and waited. "Desiree, it's Cooper. Pick up." Another pause. "I mean it. You need to call me as soon as possible. We need to talk about this." He ended the call.

The front door opened.

Her mom and dad stepped out. A handsome couple in their fifties, both were in khakis, sneakers and island print shirts. "I'm sorry, hon, but we are going to have to get a move on if we want to get to Dallas in time for our flight," Carol Lockhart said.

Jillian looked at Cooper and explained. "They're going to Hawaii for a much-deserved seven-day vacation cruise of all the islands."

Cooper smiled his congratulations. "Bon voyage."

"Thanks," her beaming parents said in unison.

Behind them the three adorable babies were visible, playing with some blocks on the living area rug in front of the sofa. Fifteen months old, they had blond hair and blue eyes. As well as Desiree's disarming smile...

Sobering, her mom turned to Jillian. "If you need to," she said, "call the department and speak with Mitzy Martin McCabe."

"I will," Jillian promised. "But it's not going to be necessary." She knew what a stand-up guy Cooper was at heart. He had proven that when he had risked his job at her parents' ranch and rescued her. She was sure he would do the right thing now. And if not, then she would, because there was no way these kids were going to end up as wards of the state, like she had. Not on her watch.

Carol paused, practical as ever. Her gaze cut to Cooper, then back to her daughter. "Help is always available if you-all find you need it," she reiterated.

Her parents hugged her and headed off.

Ready to take charge of the babies once again, Jillian walked into her home. Cooper trailed behind her while King seemed content to lounge on the shady porch, happily basking in the warm summer breeze.

Cooper paused inside the threshold, directing his gaze on her, then the kids. "So now what?" he asked.

Chapter Three

"I think we should introduce you to your nieces." Jillian sat down on the rug where they were playing. She handed a plastic block to the blond, blue-eyed angel next to her. "This is Sadie."

"Hey there, Sadie," Cooper murmured, taking a seat on the sofa opposite them. The unmistakable ache in his tone caught her unawares. Belatedly, she realized how difficult this must be for him, too.

Recognizing her name, Sadie smiled at him, and he smiled back. Seemingly unable to take his eyes from his three nieces, he leaned forward, his hands clasped between his spread knees. "How do I tell them apart?" he asked hoarsely.

Feeling both surprised and pleased by how fascinated he seemed, Jillian looked him in the eye and explained. "Well, first, they all have ID bracelets on their left wrists with their names on them. Second, even though they look identical, their personalities are quite distinct. Sadie here—" she pointed to the toddler circling the coffee table, placing toys here and there "—is in constant motion."

Cooper nodded, absorbing it all with absolute earnestness.

"Hallie," Jillian continued, "always seems to be putting something in her mouth and chewing on it."

He turned to see Hallie remove the ear of a hot pink teddy bear from her mouth and stick her first two fingers inside, instead. He winked and smiled at her. Her eyes twinkled in response.

Jillian turned to the baby girl who climbed onto her lap and snuggled close. She stroked the fine curls on her head, explaining, "Tess is the quiet one."

Interest lit his brown eyes. "They talk?"

Maybe he'd be a better uncle than she knew. Jillian suddenly felt glad he had been given the opportunity to bond with the new members of his family. "In one-word spurts. When Desiree was here, Sadie wanted her *blanket* and Hallie wanted her *teddy.*"

"What did Tess ask for?"

The tenderness in his expression made him all the more handsome, which had a thrill shooting through her. Being alone with him suddenly seemed like a dangerous proposition to her way-too-vulnerable heart. Taking an equalizing breath, she admitted, "Nothing yet. She may be a little on the shy side, too."

He picked up a block and held it out. Sadie toddled over to get it. "Block!" she said, when her little fingers encircled it.

Hallie came over, too. Cooper handed her a block, as well. Accepting it, she chattered happily. He turned his attention back to Jillian. "Were they upset when Desiree left?"

Jillian assisted Tess when she wanted to get back up to play again, easing her off her lap. Feeling surprisingly bereft without a fifteen-month-old baby cuddled against her, she shook her head, aware that had struck her a little peculiar, too. "Oddly enough, no. They smiled when their mom hugged them and gave them a kiss, and then waved goodbye to her and went back to playing."

Cooper cocked his head. "Like it was a usual occurrence."

"They may be in day care or a playgroup program. Which would explain their ease at goodbye. They know the separation is only temporary."

"Well, they look really healthy," Cooper observed.

"Don't they?" she gave the girls an admiring glance as Tess returned to sit on her lap. Hallie climbed on, too.

Sadie walked over to stare into Cooper's eyes and hand him a toy horse. He held out his hands, as if inviting her, too, to sit with him, the way Hallie and

Tess were perched on Jillian. Restless as ever, she veered away.

Hallie took her fingers out of her mouth long enough to say, "Hungry."

Jillian glanced at her watch. "It's twelve thirty. They probably are hungry."

"Do we have anything to give them?"

We, she noted. As if they were suddenly a team. She honestly wasn't sure how she felt about that— wasn't she supposed to just hand the kids off to him and be done with the situation?

But figuring he was going to need time to make at least some arrangements, she replied as graciously as possible. "Desiree said there was baby food and formula in the tote bag."

He reached over to the end of the sofa, where it had been left, then gazed inside, noting, "Baby bottles and spoons, too."

He gave it to Jillian.

She was relieved to see there was at least several days' worth of food there. That would help. Gently, she removed the two little ones from her lap and stood, looking around. "The question is, how and where are we going to do this?"

They settled on her kitchen table, and then Jillian set out three chicken-noodle dinners, applesauce jars and toddler-sized spoons. "How about you hold two of them, and I'll hold one, and I'll feed all three," she said.

Looking both amenable and slightly ill at ease, he nodded.

She put Hallie and Tess on Cooper's lap. Then settled Sadie on hers.

Because Hallie had been the one asking for lunch, she offered her the first bite.

Hallie shut her lips and turned her head to the side, making a face.

"Think she doesn't like this kind?" Cooper asked.

"I don't know. Let's see what the other two think."

Jillian offered Sadie and Tess the chicken-noodle dinner. They both ate it hungrily.

"Maybe now that it has the sister seal of approval…"

She turned back to Hallie. Again, the baby clamped her lips shut and shook her head vigorously from side to side.

Cooper suggested, "Maybe try some applesauce?"

"Okay. It could just be she doesn't care for this." She opened up the applesauce and transferred some onto the spoon.

To her delight, Hallie took it into her mouth, but then spit it right back out, letting it dribble down her chin and over her clothes. Not about to be left out, Sadie and Tess reached for the fruit. "Hungry," Sadie said.

Tess reached and screeched as if to say she wanted some, too.

Jillian gave both girls applesauce, pausing every third time to offer some to Hallie, too.

She spit out every single bite and promptly smeared

it everywhere, including on Cooper's jaw, face and hair. And while holding two babies on his lap, there wasn't anything he could do about it.

Feeling bad for him because she had come out relatively unscathed in the food stain category, Jillian started to get up with Sadie still in her arms. "Let me get you a cloth," she said.

He shook off the offer. "Might as well wait until we're done."

Without warning, Hallie began to fuss. She twisted around Cooper's lap to glare at him. "Hungry!" she said. And then promptly burst into tears.

Meanwhile, Sadie wanted to get down, as did Tess, so they let them toddle off while Jillian rushed to get another few jars of baby food from the bag. Green beans were a failure. As were the sweet potatoes. Meanwhile, Cooper's clothes were now the same rainbow of colors as his face.

"Hungry!" Hallie sobbed harder.

"I'm just going to fix her a bottle of formula and see if that helps." Jillian rushed into the kitchen while Cooper stood and carried a wailing Hallie around, patting her gently on the back all the while.

Meanwhile, her sisters saw what was going on and toddled into the kitchen, too, dragging their blankets and teddy bears. Simultaneously yelling "Bottle!" and "Mine!"

Jillian handed the first bottle to Cooper. Hallie accepted it with a sob and began to drink greedily.

Thinking it might help calm the baby, she also got Hallie's blanket and teddy.

Soon the other two girls were settled on Jillian's lap, holding their bottles and gulping down formula, too.

The house was blissfully quiet. Eyes shut, all three slipped into sleep.

"Do you think they're going to be okay there?" Cooper asked fifteen minutes later, looking at the three babies cuddled with their blankets and teddy bears on the cushions. They had pushed the coffee table flush against the sofa and made a fence of pillows to act as a safety rail.

"Well, it's the best we can do for now," Jillian whispered back. "But you're right. We do need to discuss what your plan is."

He blinked and stepped back another pace, away from his nieces. "Plan?"

"For taking care of the triplets."

He stared at her like he had just been told he had to take an exam he had no time to study for.

Determined to help him, she forged on, throwing out suggestions. "Are you thinking about hiring a babysitter or two to help you out? Or contacting someone from the Laramie Multiples Club...?"

The stunned look on his face turned to raw panic. "I don't know anything about babies. Period."

This was no time to offer excuses! The kids were

here. His help had been requested. The time for action was now.

"And yet," she said, complimenting him, in a way she hoped would reassure him that he could indeed do this, "you have a natural touch with them."

He shut his eyes briefly, looking more overwhelmed than ever. Still pondering. "Not helping."

Panic beginning to sink in for her, too, she asked, "What would help?"

It was never a good idea to overthink things. Better to just jump in and do.

He shoved a hand through his hair, looking completely at a loss. "At this point? For Desiree to come back!"

Pushing aside her simmering frustration, she said kindly, "Well, as I said, that's likely not going to happen, not for a few days at least."

Which meant the two of them had to come up with a plan now. She could not bow out until that was done.

The silence stretched uncomfortably. She began to feel a little sorry for him. From her nearly two years in foster care before she and her siblings had been adopted by the Lockharts, she knew what it was like to be thrown into an emotional situation without any warning. How scary it was to feel completely out of your depth.

"Look, I told your sister I would help care for the girls until such time that you can do it on your own. So that offer still stands." Jillian gulped, hoping she wasn't making a mistake. "But if you would prefer that I find someone else to assist you—"

He exhaled roughly. "The girls are my responsibility, not yours," he cut in. Determined, it seemed, to do the honorable thing. Just as she had expected! Even if he didn't seem to know how to go about it, or where to start.

Aware there was no time to waste, since they had no idea how long the babies were going to sleep, she clasped his biceps and drew him a little farther away, so they could talk without fear of waking the triplets. She gazed up at him. As the silence stretched out between them, she scrutinized him, the way he had once scrutinized her. Sensing there was a lot more going on in that handsome head of his—emotions she needed to know—than he was willing to admit, she pushed aside her reaction to his ultramasculine presence. And persisted. "But you do realize you're going to need help, at least initially."

If Desiree hadn't had any for fifteen long months, Jillian mused, it was no wonder she was running away. At least temporarily…

He clenched his jaw. "No kidding I'm going to need assistance!"

"So…?" she prodded.

He appeared to be mentally running down his options. Looking as uncomfortable receiving her help as she was offering it. "You'd do this for me?"

Jillian looked at the sweetly sleeping trio and felt her heart swell.

She always pretended otherwise, because she didn't want people feeling sorry for her single, childless state, but she loved babies. So much... Even though it probably wasn't in the cards for her to have a family of her own. Not unless she found the kind of life-altering love her parents and her happily wed siblings had.

And yet, these little darlings were definitely in need...

As was Cooper. Temporarily, anyway.

Already warning herself not to get too emotionally involved, she swallowed. "Sure."

Cooper's sable gaze narrowed. "Just your way of be neighborly?" he asked warily.

"That's right," she answered with a nod. Although this part was hard to admit, it needed to be said. "And because—" Jillian drew a bolstering breath "—*maybe* it's time you and I try to forget all about what happened ten years ago and call a truce."

No doubt about it. This August day was full of surprises, Cooper thought. "I'd like to try to put the past behind us, too," he said finally.

She met his gaze equably. "Then consider it a mutual goal." She moved past him briskly. "Meanwhile, we have got to get more baby gear than a suitcase and a trio of car seats if we're going to adequately care for the girls. Luckily, I know where we can borrow some. So, if you'll just give me a minute..."

Pulling her cell phone out of the pocket of her

shorts, she walked to the front door. She stepped outside to make a call, while he watched from inside.

King stood and stretched and walked over to where she sat perched on the chain-hung swing. She reached over to pet him while she talked.

It wasn't surprising his dog liked her. King was a great judge of character who gravitated toward decency and kindness. The grown-up Jillian had both traits in abundance.

Finished, she stood and gestured for King to follow her inside. He selected a place next to the air conditioner vent and settled back down to sleep. Apparently leery of waking the sleeping babies, Jillian motioned for Cooper to follow her into the kitchen, where the mess from lunch remained.

She dampened a paper towel with water and handed it to him. Belatedly, he realized he still had dried baby food on his face, the back of one hand and his clothes. He washed up, then rinsed the paper towel out again, and began working on the stains on his shirt and jeans. By the time he'd finished, she'd put the baby spoons in the dishwasher, the leftover food in the fridge.

"So, what did you manage to work out?" he asked.

Looking beautiful and capable and elusive as all get-out, Jillian hunkered down in front of the kitchen cabinet, beneath the sink, and brought out two bottles of spray cleaner. One meant for the wood floor. Another countertops and appliances.

She handed him the latter and more paper towels.

She took the other and knelt to tackle the rainbow-colored globs on the wood floor. "My parents already told me we could borrow whatever we needed from them. So my sister Faith and my brother Gabe's wife, Susannah, are driving out to Rosehaven now. They will watch the kids while you and I dash over to my folks' ranch and pack up some high chairs and Pack 'n Plays for the girls to sleep in. We can also get a few more toys, and a stroller, and maybe even a couple of baby carriers."

Unable to help but note the way the opening of her blouse gaped open slightly as she worked, revealing the uppermost curves of her breasts, Cooper forced his attention back to the task at hand and asked, "What do you mean, baby carrier?"

Her eyes gleamed. "It's like a backpack that you wear that you can put a baby in. I'm sure you've seen them." She moved closer, inundating him with the fragrance of her perfume.

He had.

He had just never imagined himself wearing one and or carting around a baby that way.

She did not seem averse to the idea, however. Which was odd, given the way she had always declared that she was happy just being an aunt to her nieces and nephews.

"BabyBjörns."

Abruptly, Cooper felt like he'd just gotten a seat on a runaway train. One that was way too domestic and intimate for comfort. He cocked his head, wondering how they had gone from making-do with what they had for a very temporary babysitting gig, to setting up a fully equipped childcare. "You really think we will need all that?" he asked skeptically.

She scoffed at his ignorance and her lovely lips formed a know-it-all grin. "And more."

Twenty minutes later, Susannah's and Faith's vehicles turned into the lane. Because the girls were still sleeping, Jillian and Cooper met them on the porch. King trailed behind.

"Thanks for coming." She hugged her sister-in-law and sister in turn.

"Happy to assist." Susannah smiled, looking every bit the pulled together Texas mom. "I'll have to leave by three, though. I have to pick up the quintuplets at school."

"Not to worry," Faith said. "I can stay for however long you need me." Since being widowed the previous February, she volunteered whenever she could. She said it helped mitigate the loss. Jillian understood the benefits of keeping busy.

She had done the same the two times she had suffered a broken heart.

"Appreciate the help." Cooper greeted the women warmly.

They smiled at him, too. Jillian accompanied the women inside, to show them where everything was. When she walked back out, Cooper was already standing next to his truck, King at his side. The two of them looked incredibly handsome in the Texas sunshine. Both of them so big and male and strong. They were the perfect representation of a man and his dog. The bond between them was unmistakable.

For a moment, she envied their closeness and constant companionship.

At times like this, she wondered if maybe she should get a pet. Maybe then she wouldn't feel so lonely.

With effort, she pushed her wistfulness aside.

"Think we should stop by your place so we can figure out what you're likely to need?" she asked.

He paused, an indecipherable look crossing his face. His reluctance faded. "Sure." He shrugged his broad shoulders affably, then pointed at the cargo area. "I need to drop off these feed blocks anyway."

She headed for her SUV. "I'll follow."

Rock Creek—Cooper's ranch—was a fifth of the size of her family's ten-thousand-acre Circle L Ranch and was still a work in progress. The pastures were nicely fenced, but the lane leading up to the house was gravel, not paved. The two-story ranch house sported pewter-gray siding and a new charcoal roof. Next to that was a renovated white barn-stable.

Cooper was already out of his truck, hefting the blocks of high protein feed and stacking them inside the barn doors, the powerful muscles in his shoulders and back flexing beneath his cotton work shirt. Watching, she felt a jolt of electricity skitter through

her. Making her unbearably aware just how uncon-
sciously sexy he was.

Finished, he met her on the front porch and led
the way inside.

Her pulse accelerating at his nearness, Jillian
crossed the threshold. Then stopped dead in her
tracks. Blinking in surprise, she propped her hands
on her hips. And murmured, "Oh…my!"

Cooper had been afraid this would be Jillian's
reaction. He watched her look around at the first
floor. It had been opened up and stripped down to
the studs. New wiring and plumbing had been put
in, as well as an HVAC system, ductwork and sec-
tions of drywall.

"Think I'm going to have a problem bringing
babies here?"

She looked at the scuffed wood floors. Then over
at the kitchen, which consisted of a temporary laundry tub sink, a hot plate, microwave and dorm fridge.
And it certainly didn't escape her attention that the
only furniture was an easy chair, a TV stand and a
comfy-looking dog bed.

"Uh, yeah." She walked over to examine a stack
of building supplies and tools. "It's pretty much a
toddler danger zone. What's upstairs?"

"Two bedrooms, one of which serves as my ranch
office, and one bath, circa 1950."

"Any of that remodeled?" she asked hopefully,
peering around the corner to see his only luxury. A

washer and dryer. She spun around on the toes of her sneakers. "Or ancient…but intact?" Her pretty eyes widened.

Abruptly aware he'd like nothing more than to take her in his arms and kiss her, he shook his head. Mouth dry, he related, "The carpet's been ripped up. And I had to take down a lot of the drywall up there to put in new plumbing and electrical."

"So, there are exposed pipes and wiring there, as well?" she asked in obvious concern.

He nodded. "I'm doing things one step at a time."

Jillian let out a breath. The look on her face reminded him that, as the daughter of Carol and Robert Lockhart, she was used to far better.

She paused thoughtfully. "What are the chances of you getting the rest of the drywall put up ASAP?"

Not good. Without a cash windfall and a team of workers willing to work double-time, anyway. Casually, he explained, "My plan was to do it as I have time." He forced himself to be even more honest. "Which, given the fact I manage a herd of two hundred cattle by myself, isn't all that often."

She had a sympathetic expression on her face, looking surprisingly understanding of his dilemma. "That's how I did my house, too, when I started Rosehaven. Initially, I put all my time and resources into the greenhouses for my roses. Getting a website up and running."

She came back to stand next to him and reached

down to pet King, her delicate hand tenderly stroking his silky head.

Cooper forced himself to concentrate on the problem before them. Where—and how—he was going to care for his three nieces. And not the soothing ministrations of her palm. Or fantasizing how that hand might feel all over him.

He shoved a hand through his hair. Thinking hard. Then he sighed. "I don't know what other choices I have, though. I'm not sure a motel room would work."

Jillian flashed him a reassuring smile. "My place will, though."

He had to admit her Victorian farmhouse was cozy, warm, safe. As appealing as the woman herself. Still, it was a lot to ask. And would have been even if they had been friends, which they weren't. Not yet, anyway. "The girls can stay there?" He wanted to make sure he understood.

Her pretty blue eyes glittering up at him, she wrapped her arms around her middle and arched a brow. Momentarily, she looked as reluctant as he felt. "You have a better idea?"

Cooper wished he had. But he didn't.

Clearly aware this situation had the potential to become very complicated for them both, Jillian paced away from him. "It's just going to be for a few days," she reminded him as they walked back outside to their vehicles.

Was it? He fell into step beside her, their bodies

so close they almost touched. "What about at night, though?" The thought of her in a sexy negligee was too alluring for comfort. Not that he had any idea what she actually wore to bed…

Unaware of the licentious direction of his thoughts, she gestured nonchalantly. "I have a guest room."

He paused, trying not to think about what it would be like to share such close quarters with her. He wanted to haul her into his arms and kiss her now. And this was after only a few hours together. What would it be like if they were together all day and all night?

He forced himself to simmer down. Reminded himself that the three babies would keep them extremely busy. Which, given the tantalizing chemistry between them, would be a very good thing. "Can I bring King?"

Interest lit her eyes, and she squared her slender shoulders. "Of course."

Cooper checked his phone again, hoping for a miracle. No text messages. Or missed calls. His spirits sank.

"Well?" Jillian asked when the silence continued to stretch between them. She stepped closer, her face turned up to his, suddenly looking a lot more relaxed.

Not only did he not have another choice…he didn't *want* another choice. Glad to be towering over her, he promised gruffly, "I'm going to do everything I can to find Desiree and get this all worked out as soon as possible." Then, well, maybe the two of them could realize their goal of ending the long-standing animosity between them and be friends. Or something more...

Jillian nodded. "Understood," she retorted softly, then checked her watch. All business once again, and ready to take on shared care of the girls, she gave his shoulder an encouraging pat. "In the meantime, we've got a lot to accomplish and very little time, so we better get a move on."

Chapter Four

It took less than five minutes for Cooper to grab King's food and dishes and pack an overnight bag. Then they set off in their respective vehicles.

This time, he followed her as she led the way to the Circle L. Inside her parents' rambling white stone ranch house, she was incredibly on task, gathering up three Pack 'n Plays, a trio of high chairs, a double and a single stroller, a basket of baby toiletries and some additional toys.

King lounged in the shade while they stowed the gear into the back of her Tahoe.

Finished, she went back into the house to see if there was anything she might have forgotten. While she was gone, Cooper tried calling Desiree again. As before, it went straight to voice mail. Unlike before, however, he tried a more gentle approach as he left his sister a message.

"Desiree, it's Cooper. First, the girls are all fine, although I know…even if they can't tell us this… that they have to miss you. So, for their sake, for *all* our sakes, please pick up the phone or call or text so we can work this out." Without warning, his voice cracked. "I'm not angry with you. Just confused." He searched for the right words. "I want to help you. The way I could never seem to before. So please, Desiree." His voice caught again. "Call. I'll have my phone on." His throat aching, he ended the call. Swore silently to himself. And couldn't help wondering if once again he had said and done the wrong thing…

With a heavy sigh, he turned to see Jillian standing silently behind him. Clearly, she had heard most, if not all, of the message he had left. Surprisingly, her eyes were glistening, too. "If I'd heard that message, I'd call," she said quietly, moving nearer.

Her silky voice caressed his skin. "Yeah. Well…" He scrubbed a hand over his face, wiping away the dampness around his eyes. "You're not Desiree."

Jillian leaned against the side of his truck, studying him from beneath a fringe of thick, dark blond lashes. "What happened between the two of you anyway?"

So much, he thought. Too much to tell in one conversation. He edged closer and caught a whiff of her perfume. Sun-drenched roses. Of course. "Our parents died in an auto accident when I was eighteen and my sister was fifteen. I talked the court into letting me be her guardian. To say it didn't go well is an understatement." His lips formed a downward slant.

He shook his head in wordless regret, recalling, "I tried my best, but…" He paused to swallow hard. "Desiree was grieving—we both were—and she wouldn't listen to anything I said."

As she listened intently, Jillian's eyes gleamed with compassion. Her empathy encouraged him to go on. "As soon as Desiree turned eighteen, she took her half of the life insurance money that was supposed to provide for our educations and ran off with her musician boyfriend." Bitter disappointment roiled in his gut. That he hadn't been able to convince his baby sister to learn from his mistakes and be more sensible.

To grow up and go to college instead of squandering her future on wildly impractical dreams and a long shot romance.

Jillian paused, seeming to catch the similarities between her own situation as a lovestruck teenager, and Desiree's. And how that had made him more determined to protect her the way he hadn't been able to protect Desiree.

She tilted her head, reflecting. "Was her boyfriend as much of a loser as Chip Harcourt?"

He caught her knowing look. "Ryan didn't have a criminal history, if that's what you're asking. But he was only eighteen, too, and as immature as she was." He folded his arms. "So, the chances of their relationship surviving once the money ran out weren't good."

Her expression gentled. "What happened after that?"

Damned if she didn't make opening up easy. Cooper exhaled. "I called her. Texted. Left messages." He scowled, remembering. "Desiree didn't answer anything. I heard from mutual friends that she and Ryan were touring with a group of musicians, trying to make it big. So—" he gestured expansively, then let his arm drop to his side "—for a while I was kind of able to keep track of her that way, and I sent messages that the door was always open if she wanted to come home." Where he could have fulfilled his promise to their parents, to always look out for his little sister.

Jillian nodded, still listening.

Cooper had always known that Jillian had a huge heart, but he had never expected that her kindness and generosity would be his soft place to fall. Even for a short time. Abruptly realizing how cathartic it was to talk about this, especially to someone so empathetic and understanding, he shrugged, and continued his story. "But you know how it is when people go their separate ways…"

"They grow apart," Jillian surmised, seeming not to judge him for that.

For a second, Cooper let himself bask in the wonder of having someone to confide in this way. It felt good to bare his soul. To unload some of the heavy burden that had been weighing him down for so long. "Anyway, eventually she stopped responding to our mutual friends' efforts to communicate, too."

"That must have been hard for you," she said softly, reaching over to lightly touch the back of his hand.

"Yeah. I worried. But I moved on, too. Finished college, took a job with your dad. Started my own ranch."

She kept her gaze locked on his. Seeming near tears. "And in all that time…"

"Nearly ten years," he told her.

"She never contacted you once?"

Pain lancing his heart, he shook his head. "Not until today." The mixture of sadness and defeat that he felt multiplied one hundred times over.

"Oh, Coop… I'm sorry." She curved her hands around his biceps. The next thing he knew she was all the way in his arms, offering a full-bodied hug of warmth and concern.

He hadn't figured on kissing her. Not here, certainly not now. Maybe not *ever*…given what had transpired between them in the past. But there was something about the way she listened to him. About the way she felt snuggled against him, about the gentle, compelling nature of her touch. For once he acted as recklessly as she once had and let everything else go—the sorrow, the grief, the guilt…the confusion over what came next—and lowered his lips to hers, laying claim. Felt her soft and slender body meld to his.

She'd been a kid when he had known her before, not much more than a teen himself.

Now, she was a woman. A strong, selfless one at that. And while he could curtail desire on its own, he could not seem to resist the feel of her soft and feminine body so close to his. The sweet seductive taste of her lips. Or the way she wound her arms about his neck and pressed her breasts against his chest, offering the physical comfort he so desperately needed.

His body hardened. And another jolt of awareness arced between them...

Jillian shuddered in response at the liquid stroking of his tongue and the unhurried pressure of his lips. He tasted so good, so delicious and intoxicatingly male. She had never been wanted like this. Never been caught up in an embrace this way. But the depth of her response to him shook her to her very soul. Excitement and desire roared through her.

This was the kiss she had always yearned to have, the kiss of her wildest dreams. The kiss of a *real man* who when it came to the pleasures in life would not hold back.

Which was why it had to stop. Now, she told herself resolutely. Before they let the emotion and shock of the day push them any further. Because, she reminded herself firmly, she was no longer the girl he had known, the girl who got swept up in the moment and acted solely on emotion. These days she ran her business and her personal life with clear-eyed determination. She did not get sidetracked into ill-fated romances that would only break her heart...

Determined to bring cool reason back to a day that had been far too disconcerting already, she broke off the kiss. Stepped back, stunned, her lips still moist from his. She drew in a stabilizing breath. Meeting his eyes directly, she reminded him, "We need to *focus* here, Coop." *On everything that needed to be done.*

Doing her best to hide her trembling, she reached into her pocket for her keys. Added, even more firmly, "My sisters and the babies are waiting on us. We have to get going."

"All right," he replied, his expression maddeningly inscrutable. And suddenly it was as if their unexpectedly intimate connection, their kiss, had never occured.

Cooper didn't know what had happened.

Jillian was the one who had a reputation for acting impulsively regarding matters of the heart. Not him. Except for that *one* time. But he had learned his lesson. Never making the same mistake since then...

He was just going to have to remember to keep his guard up.

Fortunately, their mutual drives back to Rosehaven were accomplished quickly. Once there, they busied themselves carrying the baby gear up to the porch, and then inside the house.

The triplets were awake, playing happily on the rug in the center of her living room floor. Faith and Susannah were sitting cross-legged nearby, watching over them.

Faith's phone dinged with the alert of an incoming call. Susannah looked at her in sisterly affection. "You have to answer that."

Faith snuggled Hallie and Tess close, while Sadie climbed onto Susannah's lap. "Whatever it is, it can't be as important as what we're doing now." She grinned as the girls took turns bussing the underside of her chin. She kissed the top of their heads with a loud smacking sound that made them giggle.

Watching the babies basking in the attention, Cooper smiled. Faith was such a natural with children. It was a shame she didn't have any of her own yet. Word around town was that she had always wanted kids, but her late husband hadn't wanted her to get pregnant until he was out of the military, and there to experience it with her. Sadly, a few months after Harm Hewitt had resigned from the Navy Seals, and returned to Texas to be with her, he had died in a construction accident. Leaving their unrealized dream to have a family together just that…

The ding sounded again.

Susannah persisted. "What if it's some kind of emergency?"

Faith made a face. "It's not."

"How do you know?" Susannah asked.

Faith rolled her eyes. "Because if it were a *family* emergency, they'd be calling you and Jillian, too."

She had a point, Cooper thought. The Lockharts were a tight-knit bunch.

"Still...you need to at least check," Susannah said, unexpectedly handing Sadie to Cooper. Then she rose elegantly, looking at Cooper and Jillian for support.

Figuring it was a Lockhart family matter, Cooper stayed out of it. Jillian reached down to take Hallie while Susannah did the same with Tess. "At least see what the call is about..." Jillian said.

"Fine." Faith pulled her phone out, looking down for a long moment, her face turning pale. "It's Laramie County DCFS."

All three women tensed. With a sigh, Faith rose, too. She looked as if she might cry. "I'll get this outside." She walked toward the foyer.

King, sensing Faith needed comforting, followed, tail wagging. The door shut behind them.

Susannah consulted her watch. "I have to leave in a few minutes, but if you want to go ahead and get the Pack 'n Plays set up...wherever you're going to have them."

"Upstairs," Jillian stated. She took one, while Cooper picked up the other two. Aware how intimate this was all beginning to feel, he followed Jillian as she led the way up the staircase, down the hall, past the master, guest room and bath, to an office at the end.

Out the window, they could see Faith pacing the front yard.

"Everything okay with her?" Cooper asked, trying not to notice how pretty Jillian looked in the afternoon sunlight. He wished he could kiss her again, to discover if the feel of her lips against his was as fantastic the second time around…

Jillian swung toward him, her necklace nestled in the soft swell just above her breasts. She lifted her chin. "Faith has been on the foster-to-adopt waiting list for about six months now. For the first three or four months, they refused to match her because they said it was too close to Harm's passing. But they let her go ahead and take all the classes and get approved to be a foster parent."

Cooper began unpacking the Pack 'n Plays from their canvas carrying cases. Following Jillian's lead, he opened them up from their collapsed states and locked them into place. "So why wouldn't she want to talk to DCFS when they called?"

Jillian got out the baby bed linens they'd brought and covered the mattresses with cotton sheets. "Because it seems like every time my sister gets close to being matched…a distant relative or family friend steps forward to claim the child." She released a belabored sigh. "And then she's back at square one."

"That must suck."

The twin spots of color in her cheeks made her even more gorgeous. "It does. Especially because the last thing she needs right now is a lot of ups and downs."

Realizing all over again what a smart, intuitive and magnificent woman Jillian was, Cooper asked quietly, "Then why doesn't she just wait a bit? Until she's feeling more able to handle it?" He resisted the urge to tuck a tendril of hair behind her ear.

"Because, as everyone pretty much knows, my sister's wanted a baby forever. She would have fostered sooner, had Harm let her..."

Cooper caught the low note of frustration in Jillian's voice. "He was against it?"

Jillian nodded, her soft lips compressing. She turned to look Cooper in the eye. "Harm was afraid Faith would get too attached to any and every child she cared for and, since many of the kids are only in a foster home temporarily, that Faith would get her heart broken at least once, if not more. He didn't want to see that. And he also wanted his own biological children with Faith, when the time was right." Jillian frowned and turned her glance out the window. Regret etching the pretty features of her face, she let out a beleaguered sigh. "Faith felt because they were married, she should honor Harm's wishes. Instead of pushing for what she really wanted. So, they waited."

He watched her ease around the office furniture to close the blinds against the afternoon sun. One slat clung crookedly to the window. As Jillian reached up to slide it back into place, the hem of her yellow camp shirt lifted, exposing a strip of silky midriff, right above the waistband of her shorts.

His body reacted immediately.

He shifted to lessen the pressure at the front of his jeans. And worked to keep his mind on the conversation, rather than what he would like to do at that instant. Which was act as impulsively as she always did in matters of the heart. Haul her against him and kiss her again.

He cleared his throat, watching her ease back around the furniture to stand beside the three Pack 'n Plays. "You disapprove?"

Jillian folded her arms, the action emphasizing the soft curves of her breasts. She met his gaze, seeming to choose her words carefully. "I think it's easier than most people realize for a person to run out of time. The way Harm did. The way Faith did in her marriage to him."

Cooper agreed.

Her eyes glimmered sadly. "Everybody thinks nothing bad will actually happen to them, it will always be someone else. That there will always be plenty of time to do what they want and need to do in the future."

Resisting the urge to take her in his arms, the way she had held him earlier, Cooper nodded. He saw where she was going with this. "But sometimes tragedy intervenes," he said hoarsely. "Like with the sudden deaths of my folks and yours."

"Yes." Jillian drew a deep, quavering breath. "And

before you know it your whole life has collapsed, and you're never going to have the chance to do what you thought you would."

Cooper realized how small and intimate the temporary nursery/home office was beginning to feel. He stepped back slightly, moving beneath the portal, and partway into the hallway. "Which is why Faith signed up to foster-adopt after Harm passed, instead of taking time to grieve."

Keeping her physical distance, too, Jillian leaned against the edge of her desk, one feminine ankle crossed over the other. "Faith knows that she's going to mourn her loss whether she cares for a child in need or not. But she also knows that the best way to ease an empty place in your heart is to bring more love into it."

Cooper tracked the luxurious fall of Jillian's hair. Checking the urge to touch the silky strands, he returned his attention to the flushed contours of her face and asked, "So what does any of that have to do with Faith not wanting to answer her phone? Or being upset about hearing from DCFS?"

Jillian revealed with cautious enthusiasm, "Faith had a call earlier this week, about an infant this time…"

"So?" Cooper still didn't understand.

Jillian shrugged her slender shoulders and emotion flickered in her eyes. She stepped closer, speaking even more quietly. "Faith probably thinks they are going to tell her they don't need her again, and she wasn't ready to hear it. Anyway—" she led the way back down the hall "—there's the guest room." It had a comfortable-looking queen-size bed and a dresser, and was decorated in the subtle pastels she favored. She pointed in the opposite direction. "You can use the bath across the hall." She paused. "I have my own in the master suite."

Her house, nice as it was, suddenly seemed awfully small. And *way* too cozy. This situation was complicated enough already. He was just going to have to be careful to keep his distance. Even if her sisters and the babies were around to chaperone. "Thanks," he said, struck again by just how kind and generous Jillian was. He had really underestimated her all these years by not getting to know her better.

He wanted to change that now.

They descended the stairs, with her in the lead, just as Faith came back in, her face flushed and stained with tears. "You're never going to believe it!" she cried happily. "I've finally been matched! With a two-month-old infant, no less! They need me to drive to San Angelo right away!"

Jillian and Susannah beamed with excitement and hugged her. "That's wonderful!"

Faith stepped back, still looking a little dazed. "But I won't be able to help you, Jillian…at least not the way I planned," she warned in a worried tone.

"It's okay," Jillian said, once again putting the needs of others above her own. "Cooper and I have this." She turned to him and delivered a long, meaningful look. "Don't we, cowboy?"

He gazed back at her, looking into her gorgeous blue eyes. Knowing there was only one answer to give, even if he didn't know the first thing about taking care of babies. He dipped his head in acknowledgment, exuding confidence. "We sure do, darlin'. We sure do…"

Chapter Five

"I think we're in over our heads here," Cooper said several hours later, as they confronted the after-dinner mess, and the prospect of baths and bedtime that awaited them.

Wasn't that just like a man when presented with a domestic dilemma! "No, we're not," Jillian said. She placed her hands on her hips, surveying the three adorable little baby girls, sitting side by side in their high chairs. All were busy trying to get Cheerios to their mouths and had no idea that they had baby food and mashed banana smeared on their faces and in their hair. "We just need a system."

Cooper chuckled as all three began to bang their sippy cups of milk on their high chair trays. The corners of his sensual lips turning up while the cacophony increased; he turned back to her. "I'm listening."

"If I have learned anything from my siblings with multiples, it's that when it comes to caring for more than one child simultaneously, doing everything by assembly line is key."

Cocking a brow, he turned to let his eyes drift over her lazily. "Makes sense." He lounged against the counter, the picture of masculine virility. "How do you want to start?"

She wasn't used to being around quite so much testosterone. Never mind in the cozy confines of her home. Warmth spiraled through her veins and made its way into her cheeks.

Her heartbeat accelerating, she circled around the counter. Reminded herself that the kiss they had shared was a one-off, and the most they would ever be was friends borne out of necessity, and probably only for a short while, at that. Finding her throat a little dry, she refilled her iced tea glass and offered him the same. Their fingers brushed as she handed him his tumbler. She ignored the tingling sensation. "I suggest we set up a bath station at the kitchen sink. I'll bathe them. You can wrap them in bath towels and hold them afterward. Then, when we get all three done, we'll take them upstairs to my bed, lay them down there, and get them dressed all at once."

Cooper nodded, then their glances clashed once again. He smiled. "Sounds like a plan."

A plan, Jillian thought in relief, that would keep

her so busy she would have no more time to notice
just how ruggedly handsome and masculine he was.

Luckily, the girls liked having their hair sham-
pooed and playing in the warm sudsy water. They
savored being held against Cooper's broad chest even
more.

"So what's next?" he asked when they had finished diapering and dressing all three.

Watching him tenderly cradle his nieces, Jillian
realized what a good daddy he would be one day.

"We cuddle with them a little bit, then gather up
their teddy bears and blankets and tuck them in."

"Think they're going to go to sleep?"

Given how tired but alert they looked? "I hope
so," Jilian said. "They've had a pretty long day."

Cooper furrowed his brow, thinking. "Maybe it
would help if we rocked them."

She sent him a bemused look. "Except I don't
have a rocker. Never mind one that would accommodate all three."

"You've got a porch swing."

She let out a slow breath. "True." And the breeze
that blew across the front porch this time of evening
was really nice. She picked up Hallie, while he gathered up Sadie and Tess. Together, they made their
way outside and settled side by side on the porch
swing. King lay at their feet. Cooper smelled ap-
pealingly like baby soap and shampoo. She imagined she did, too.

As they swung back and forth, he nodded at the

neat rows of greenhouses. "What made you decide to grow roses?" he asked quietly as the girls snuggled contently in their arms.

"My first mom was into gardening. She especially loved the antique roses that were there when she and my dad purchased their home in Houston. She spent hours cultivating them and bringing them back to life."

Cooper pushed the swing lightly with his foot. The gentle back and forth motion was almost as lulling as the feel of his body so close to hers. His gaze moved over her, igniting wildfires wherever it landed. "Do you still have any of them now?"

"No." Jillian felt some of the barriers around her heart begin to lower. Sadly, she told him, "The flower bushes were lost in the fire after our home got struck by lightning when I was a kid."

Cooper paused. "Is that how you lost your folks?"

Jillian recalled the terrible thunderstorm with shattering clarity. "Yes. At first it had seemed like everything was going to be okay, since the blaze was contained to the attic."

Unable to touch her with their arms full of drowsy babies, he pressed his knee to hers instead. "Then what happened?" he asked her.

Jillian swallowed. "My parents got all eight of us kids safely out and across the street to a neighbor's. The rain seemed to have put out the fire so they went back into the house to get the safe that contained the valuables when the gas water heater exploded, killing them instantly."

He exhaled roughly. "How old were you at the time?"

"Seven."

"Wow. That's rough."

It had been. Jillian nodded.

Kindness exuded from him. Again, he pressed his knee to hers, in lieu of a hug that she imagined he might have offered had his arms been free. "I'm sorry," he said fiercely.

His heartfelt empathy meant a lot. Jillian ignored the pressure behind her eyes. "Thanks." Her voice was hoarse, too.

For a moment they swung in silence, their gazes turned to the babies in their arms, who were now having trouble keeping their eyes open, and then they both looked out at the horizon. "And that's how you ended up with Carol and Robert Lockhart?" Cooper asked.

"Eventually," Jillian admitted, aware how good it felt to be out here with him like this. Having the girls snuggled with them, well, that was an added bonus.

Aware that Cooper seemed to want to hear more about what she had been through, and cognizant of the fact that it was something she rarely spoke of, and probably needed to do more of, Jillian sighed. Forced herself to open up a little more. "Initially, we were all split up and put into foster care. It was about two years before we were all reunited. But," she added, seeing the depth of concern in his eyes, "you're right. My four brothers and three sisters and I have Carol and Robert to thank for that. They didn't give up until they had adopted all of us."

They rocked some more. The horizon turned streaky with pink and gray and blue. Overhead, dusk settled around them like a gauzy blanket. "What was foster care like?" Cooper asked.

Jillian shrugged. Something else she didn't like to talk about. "Hard. Lonely."

He shifted, so he could better see her face, his thigh pressing against hers. "You didn't like your foster parents?"

She shifted, too. Feeling Hallie sigh and burrow more deeply into her chest, as she moved toward him. Abruptly, she realized there was so much more to Cooper Maitland than she had ever let herself see before. She regretted their undeserved ambivalence toward each other, all these years. "I wouldn't let myself like my foster parents."

His gaze sifted over her. "How come?"

Tess dropped her head to one muscular shoulder, turning her face to his neck. On his other side, Sadie did the same. The scene was so right and warm, tender and familial it made Jillian want to weep.

Aware Cooper was still waiting for her explanation, she admitted thickly, "I didn't want another family. I wanted the one I'd had. Before the fire. My foster parents couldn't understand that. They thought

I should be grateful. More willing to fit in. So the situation was…polite, I guess, but cold."

"Sounds tough."

It had been. To the point she didn't want to go back there again, even in memory. She shrugged in an offhand manner. "It all worked out in the end."

"True."

Another silence fell. Cooper continued rocking them all back and forth. The first fireflies could be seen in the descending darkness.

Not done probing her psyche, Cooper stared at her thoughtfully. "Is this why you don't want to marry and have kids?"

Jillian blinked, surprised by the question. "How do you know that?" she demanded, a little embarrassed.

He chuckled. "Everyone knows that. Guys talk about which women want to get married, which don't."

"Ah." She joshed him right back, observing archly, "And you hang out with the women who don't."

It was his turn to shrug. "I'm not going to pretend my ranch and my dog aren't my first priority."

Aware what a natural Cooper was with babies, whether he realized it yet or not, she studied him curiously. "And that's okay with most women or it's not?"

He winced. "Not, mostly."

Hmm. "Have you ever been serious about anyone?" she queried.

"Here in Laramie County?"

Why did she have the feeling that was a trick question on his part? That he was suddenly parsing the information he was willing to give out to her. Although she supposed it didn't really matter what he had or hadn't done back in high school and college. She certainly didn't want her mistakes at that time to matter now. "Yes." She clarified her question with an an inquisitive smile. "Since you have lived here in Laramie County."

His big body relaxed next to hers. "I had two casual relationships that ended when the women I was seeing wanted more."

Funny, she was a little jealous imagining him with another woman. Although why that should be, she didn't know. She studied the crinkles around his eyes. Finding them every bit as sexy and appealing as the rest of him. Noticing all three of the kids were now sound asleep, she let her voice drop to just above a whisper. "More being…?"

He cocked his head. "Marriage, kids."

She felt another emotional hit she did not expect. Maybe because she was beginning to see that by assuming she didn't need a husband or kids of her own, that just being an aunt would be enough, she was selling herself short. "You don't want that?"

His gaze narrowed. "Not then I didn't."

Jillian wet her lips, her heart skipping a beat. Why was it that being here with him and the kids, like this, suddenly made her able to see herself with a happy, tight-knit family of her very own? A dream that had always eluded her...

"And now...?" she prodded, wondering if he were suddenly as in touch with his paternal side as he appeared? "What do you want for your future?" *What did she want?*

Was just being a doting aunt going to be enough?

He paused, struggling to find an answer. "I don't know." Appearing ready to move on from their intimate talk, he looked at the sweetly slumbering babies. "Think we should put them down now?" he whispered.

Although they were all so cozy she hated to get up, Jillian agreed. "Absolutely."

They rose carefully and went up the staircase to the second floor. They eased the babies into their Pack 'n Plays, placing their teddy bears and blankets next to them.

Jillian turned on the baby monitor she had borrowed from her parents. Then they eased from the room.

Back downstairs, they gravitated to the kitchen, where the dinner and bath mess awaited them. Cooper surveyed the dried glops of baby food on the high chairs, floors and even a couple of places on the wall. "I can clean this up," he said.

Jillian's stomach rumbled, reminding her it had been hours since she'd had anything to eat herself. "Why don't we both do it," she suggested, "and then I'll see if I can rustle up something for us to eat. That is—" she paused, wondering just how discerning a houseguest he was going to be "—if you're okay with leftovers?"

Not everyone was.

His grin was as wide as all Texas. "Thanks," he rumbled. "Sounds great."

Cooper'd had reservations about sharing the caretaking responsibilities of the triplets with Jillian. Not that he'd had much choice. He hadn't figured that two people who had once mixed about as well as oil and water would be able to get along, especially in a high-pressure situation. So he was surprised by how well they worked together. First, in feeding, bathing and putting the babies to sleep. Then as they made short work of the kitchen cleanup.

More fascinating still was how easily they had fallen into synch with each other.

He had once assumed she was not his type, and he certainly wasn't hers.

Now he was pretty sure he'd been wrong.

Although how he would convince her of that, he did not yet know.

Loving the easy way she moved about her warm and comfy kitchen, he watched her take out containers filled with multiple servings of turkey meat loaf, mashed potatoes and gravy and green beans. "You cook like this all the time?" he asked curiously, aware it all looked sumptuous enough to be on a magazine cover.

She eased past him, still smelling like the baby shampoo and soap that clung to them both. She paused to rummage through a drawer, giving him a fine view of her curvaceous backside in the process.

She pulled out a spatula, slotted spoon and gravy ladle. Then closed the door with a sexy swivel of her hip. "I either do something supersimple, like a salad or an omelet for dinner," she told him as she stretched her arm to reach two dinner plates, then set them on the counter, next to the food.

"Or—" her face brightened with the wattage of her genuine smile "—I cook a real meal and then have it for several nights in a row." She made an off-handed gesture. "Sort of depends on how busy I am." She filled two stoneware plates, covered them with waxed paper, and then put them into the microwave one after the other to reheat.

He leaned against the counter, hands braced on either side of him, watching her.

She brought out the pitcher of iced tea. Then handed him two glasses and silverware. "What about you?" she asked casually.

He set their places at the table. Aware this was something else they had in common. "I do the same thing, although my multimeal entrées are usually takeout of some sort, bought whenever I happen to be in town. Pizza, barbecue, Tex-Mex."

"Ah, the life of a bachelor..."

He studied the lively color in her high, sculpted

cheeks. "No kidding. Although at least you have a full kitchen in which to work," he teased.

"Yeah," she chuckled sympathetically, "you really are down to the bare bones culinary workspace at Rock Creek."

To date, he'd been in no hurry to fix that.

Now, he saw there could be a benefit to a full, working kitchen. When it came to having company...

The microwave pinged a second time, and they sat down with their plates.

He savored his first bite of turkey meat loaf smothered in rich gravy. Shook his head in surprise as the taste of fresh sage, celery and onion hit his tongue. Damn, it was good. Maybe the best thing he'd ever eaten. "This tastes like Thanksgiving," he said, praising her with a contented smile.

Jillian waggled her brows. "That's because I put everything that goes into stuffing into it."

He continued eating with enthusiasm. He'd forgotten what it was like to sit down with a woman and enjoy a home-cooked meal together. Even if she hadn't known he would be there to enjoy it when she had initially prepared the delicious food. "Well, it's amazing."

She returned his glance shyly, appearing touched by the compliment. "Thank you."

He reached across the table to grasp her hand. "It's me who should be thanking you," he said gruffly. "For helping out with my nieces."

"I'm happy to help, Cooper. I mean that."

He knew it. Felt it. Appreciated it. Which made him want to take her in his arms and kiss her all over again.

Not that complicating matters that way would be a good thing.

Abruptly, King got to his feet. They all heard the sound of an engine cutting off, and then a vehicle door shutting. From where they sat, they could see out the windows that overlooked the front porch. And saw a uniformed deputy stepping out of a Laramie County Sheriff's patrol car.

Too late, Cooper realized he should have warned Jillian.

"I wonder what's going on," she murmured in concern. King's haunches stiffened in alert, and he walked over to stare meaningfully at his owner to inform him that they had company.

"It's okay, boy, we've got it." Cooper petted his dog, glad King'd had the sense not to *bark* the alarm. He walked with Jillian to the front door, adding casually, "I asked Dan McCabe to come by."

They all knew each other. As well as being about the same age as Cooper and Jillian, Dan was one of the deputies who had been on the scene when Jillian's illicit elopement was thwarted and Chip Harcourt was arrested.

At the question in her pretty blue eyes, Cooper explained, "I wanted to talk with him about Desiree. And since you're the one who actually spoke with her this morning, I thought you should probably be there, too."

She stopped him, a hand on his forearm. "Are you *sure* you want to involve law enforcement?"

No. But he didn't know what else to do under the circumstances. "Don't worry. I'm not trying to get my sister in trouble."

Jillian looked skeptical, but with Dan about to ring the doorbell—and possibly wake the triplets—there was no time to talk about it. She drew a deep breath as they walked out onto the front porch. Dan lifted a brow at the sight of them together, side by side, their body language indicating that whatever this was, they were in it together.

Too late, Cooper realized that the deputy was as aware, same as just about everyone else in Laramie County, that Cooper and Jillian hadn't exactly been friends. Up until today anyway…

"So," Dan drawled, "you two finally kissed and made up."

Jillian blushed. "Not exactly."

Actually, Cooper thought, that was exactly what they had done. At least in *his* opinion.

The lawman raised his brow. Waited with the legendary McCabe good humor and kindness.

Cooper gestured for them all to have a seat on the front porch, then said, "It's about my younger sister, Desiree Maitland." He went on to explain what had happened. Including the fact they hadn't been able to get in touch with her since she had left the triplets at

Rosehaven. "And I really need to find her," Cooper told him. "See what's really going on with her and try and work things out."

"Well, it's too soon for a missing person report. And that wouldn't be appropriate, anyway, given what you've told me. That she asked Jillian to watch her kids, in what appears to be an emergency situation, until you showed up. Which you did."

"Can you at least run a background check on her? And come up with a current address or something more than what we've got right now, which is just her cell phone number?" Cooper persisted.

Dan shook his head. "Not through the sheriff's department, not without starting an official report. Which we don't want to do because that would immediately trigger the Department of Children and Family Services involvement. And could end up with the triplets being put into the foster care system as soon as tonight."

"Which we really don't want," Jillian said anxiously. "Because once in, it's hard to get out."

Dan nodded his agreement. "Right. But I do have a private investigator friend who owes me a favor. If you have Desiree's birth date and social security number, I can give him a call. See what he can find out."

Luckily, Cooper knew both by heart. He recited them for the lawman, who wrote them down. "How long will it take?"

Dan made a seesawing motion. "If he's near his

computer, I might be able to have something by the end of my shift at nine. I could call you then."

It felt like the longest hour of Cooper's life. Together, he and Jillian finished their dinner and did their dishes. While she started a load of baby laundry—because the triplets didn't have many clothes with them—he took King out for a walk around the property. Finally, around nine fifteen, Dan McCabe called. "I was able to get a current address for you. It's an apartment complex in Dallas."

Cooper jotted down the information. "Anything else?"

"She's divorced. Doesn't appear to be regularly employed. Maybe you should start there. And see what else you can uncover."

"Thanks," Cooper said gratefully. "I will."

He hung up to see Jillian standing beside him. Quickly, he filled her in. "What do you want to do?" she asked, her expression intent.

That was easy. "Go to Dallas as soon as possible."

She did not look surprised. "You want me to handle the triplets while you're gone?" she asked, resting her hands on her hips.

"No." He knew it was a big ask, but he went ahead anyway. "I want you all to go with me."

Chapter Six

"Think we should each pack a bag?" Cooper asked the following morning. He had risen earlier than any of them. Shaving and showering. Putting on a tan button-up shirt and jeans. Which left her wondering just what he had slept in the night before. Since they hadn't seen each other since they'd checked on the sweetly slumbering babies and said good-night around 11:00 p.m.

Not that she should be wondering about his bedtime attire...

Trying not to notice how handsome he looked or good he smelled, like a sun-drenched forest after a hard summer rain, she doled out sippy cups of milk and dry cereal to the triplets who were in their high chairs.

Because she hadn't thought to get an early start, she was still wearing the knit pajama T-shirt and sleep shorts she had worn to bed. And while the cotton clothing covered the same amount of skin as her regular day clothing, she still felt a little vulnerable.

Not that Cooper seemed to notice...

With effort, she forced her attention back to the conversation at hand, instead of what his sexy, masculine presence was doing to her. "I think it's a good idea for us to pack some extra clothes for everyone, even if we end up driving back to Laramie County later today. Since babies are notorious for getting everything they get on themselves on their 'handlers.'"

He grinned and sat down to spoon-feed the triplets cereal and fruit baby food, while she set about making some breakfast for the two of them, as well.

His brow furrowed. "What do you think about possibly staying the night in Dallas...if it seems like that might help?"

Jillian warmed some precooked sausage in the skillet and broke half a dozen eggs into a bowl. He was right. They didn't know what they were walking into. All Desiree had said when she'd left the triplets at Rosehaven was that something had come up, and she needed her brother to watch his nieces. The implication had been *temporarily*. But Desiree hadn't been specific, even when Jillian had pressed her. Only saying she wasn't sure. But that Cooper "owed her that at least. And much more..."

Something, she recalled, that Cooper had seemed to agree with.

She whisked the eggs with a little cream, then poured them into a skillet already lined with melted butter. She pivoted to face the man directly. "I'm fine with whatever we need to do to help you resolve this family crisis."

He paused to wipe three chins with a soft cloth before their faces became a huge mess, as they had the night before. And went back to feeding, one after the other. "Thanks."

Aware this was what mornings would feel like if she ever did marry and have kids, she turned to smile at his regal yellow Lab, who was lounging in a pool of sunshine, streaming in through the breakfast room windows. "What about King?"

Cooper sent his dog an affectionate glance. He was rewarded with a happily thumping tail. "I've got a friend coming by to pick him up in an hour."

Next question. "Do you want to take my Tahoe or your pickup truck?" She plated their breakfasts, handed him his and sat down opposite him. As she settled in her chair, their knees brushed briefly beneath the table, causing a jolt of desire to course through her.

He flashed her a genial grin. "If you don't mind, your Tahoe would probably be better since it sits eight and my pickup truck only holds five."

Her heartbeat picked up. "You're hoping Desiree will come back with us?"

"Yeah." He ate his breakfast with pleasure. "Assuming she's there…and not off with that guy you saw with her when she dropped the kids off."

Jillian knew that was a possibility, too. On the other hand, she hadn't gotten any kind of intimate vibe between Desiree and the driver of the Lexus.

So he could have been just a friend or an associate. There was really no way to tell.

"Well, hopefully she will be there when we get to Dallas."

Except, as it turned out, Cooper's sister was not in her apartment when they all arrived shortly after noon.

Or at least she didn't answer his knock on the door, any more than she had answered any of their phone calls or texts.

"What now?" Jillian asked Cooper when he strolled back to her Tahoe. The vehicle was parked in front of a townhome-style apartment in a sprawling family-friendly complex, common to the metro area.

The engine was running, the air conditioner on. She had let him drive, so she was in the passenger seat. The triplets were all in their car seats. After long naps and a two-and-half-hour car ride, they were getting restless.

Cooper shrugged his broad shoulders. "Maybe we should go over to the rental office, talk to the manager on duty."

Fortunately, the office was only another building over. They opened up the double and single strollers they had borrowed from her mom, strapped the babies in and headed that way.

A petite woman with olive skin and shiny black hair, drawn into a sleek bun, greeted them when they walked in. Seeing the triplets, she broke into a wide grin of recognition. She looked at Cooper. "You must be Desiree's brother! She said you would probably be stopping by sometime in the next few days." The manager reached into a drawer and produced an envelope. "She left this for you. The key to her place is inside." She paused to kneel in front of the babies and greet each of them in turn, then reluctantly rose, facing Cooper and Jillian once again. "Let me know if there is anything I can assist you with regarding the move out."

Move out?

The two of them exchanged astonished looks.

"It needs to happen by Friday," the manager continued.

Two days from then.

"But obviously you know that, which is why you're here," the woman said.

Actually, they hadn't known any of this, but sensing Cooper did not want to get into a private family matter with someone he did not know, she simply nodded then promised, "Will do. Thanks."

He wheeled the double stroller back out the door. Jillian followed with the single stroller. The August sun was getting really warm. The triplets were happy when they entered the cool air of the apartment they called home. Seeing where they were, they waved their arms in excitement, babbling and demanding to get down to play with their toys, which were in the corner of the living area. Jillian and Cooper quickly moved to accommodate them, then he sat down to read the handwritten letter. He scanned it, his expression inscrutable, then handed it over to her to read.

Dear Coop,
If you are reading this, it means you've shown up, as I figured you would. Sorry everything was so rushed, and we didn't have time to discuss any of this first, but I also knew if we did, you would try and talk me out of what I know have to do. So…

My friend Darcy—the registered nurse next door—can help you with anything you need. You should take all of the girls' things. My music and clothes and guitars and the daybed, if you don't mind, too. (It's a good luck charm for me.) The rest of the furniture, dishes and so on can all be boxed up and donated to the Angel Fund, which helps single moms. Card enclosed. Just call them and they'll send a crew over to pick it all up.

I have to vacate the premises by Friday at 5:00 p.m. Move out cleaning has already been arranged. Just leave the key with the apartment complex manager and she will take care of the rest.

Hopefully, I'll be able to get to Laramie to pick up my stuff in two to four weeks. If you could stow it for me until then, I would appreciate it.

Desiree

"Wow," Jillian said.

"Yeah, wow," he agreed. His expression grim, he turned to look her in the eye. "I guess this isn't going to be the short-term babysitting gig I was hoping for."

She felt for him. He had a right to be stunned and overwrought. This situation was getting more out of control by the moment. For all their sakes, she tried to look on the bright side. "It could just be two weeks."

The grooves on either side of his mouth deepened. "Or four."

Jillian went over to check diapers. All three were damp. She picked up Hallie and Sadie and handed them to him, then gathered Tess in her arms. "That's still just a month," she said soothingly. "In the meantime, why don't we look around a little, see what we're really dealing with?"

The kitchen and breakfast room were open to the living area, and situated at the rear of the townhome's first floor. A safety gate blocked off the stairs. The second floor held two rooms and a bath. The nursery barely had room for three mismatched cribs, side by side, and a single changing table–dresser. The "master" held a daybed, recording equipment, crates of handwritten music and several guitars. Autographed posters, a few featuring Desiree, alone, others with a couple of different bands, adorned the wall. Country-western costumes hung in the closet beside a variety of jeans, vests, fancy boots and belts and pretty guitar straps. It was the lair of a disciplined musician.

Jillian drew a deep breath. "Did you know she was this dedicated to her craft?"

He looked shocked. "I had no idea," he murmured, shaking his head.

Aware the girls still needed to be changed, Jillian led the way back into the nursery. She set Tess on the changing table and reached for a clean diaper. Using the same assembly-line process they had used the evening before, they diapered all three.

"Think they are hungry?" Cooper asked.

Jillian consulted her watch. "They must be." It had been five hours since breakfast.

The kitchen held frozen dinners, baby food, a carton of unopened milk that was still fresh and a variety of baby finger food. There were three mismatched high chairs, which looked secondhand.

They settled the girls into their high chairs. She got out three spoons and three jars of chicken-and-vegetable baby food. Cooper fed them in turn while Jillian filled the sippy cups with milk, then sat down to assist. Finally, the girls were all fed—even Hallie, who hadn't wanted to eat at first—and continued sitting in their chairs while putting apple and whole grain teething biscuits into their mouths, and then rubbing them across their gums.

Jillian turned to Coop, marveling at how quickly they were getting into the "parenting routine." "You must be famished, too," she observed.

He ran a hand over his face, admitting finally, "You're right. We probably do need to eat, too."

"Well, let's see what we've got." Jillian went through the options in the freezer. Pulled out a steak and potato meal for him, a mac and cheese entrée for herself. She microwaved both simultaneously, while he got them each a bottle of water. Together, they sat down to eat.

"What are you thinking?" she asked.

He pulled out his phone, checked it again. Nothing from Desiree. Jillian didn't have anything, either.

He sat back in his chair, his expression conflicted. "Despite everything, a part of me is impressed with my baby sister, that she has managed all this for as long as she has."

He was right, Jillian noted in admiration.

"This place is clean. Well-organized." She listed all the things he could be grateful for and proud of. "Desiree's obviously been working hard to establish a career. Her letter to you showed a lot of thought and concern, too."

His jaw clenching abruptly, he pushed away from the table. "But dumping the kids the way she did, did not."

Unless Desiree'd felt she had no choice.

Because of whatever it was she'd had to do...

But had been reluctant to talk to Cooper about, because she'd expected he would not understand...

Which he clearly didn't...

She watched him stalk to the sink, rinse out the small plastic tray. Not wanting the girls to notice how upset he was, she moved to his side. Then turned so her back was to the sink, her face slanted toward his. "So. Now that we know the situation. What do you want to do?" she asked.

"I don't know." He watched her rinse out her own tray, then dropped both into the recycling bin. Pacing back to her side, he stopped abruptly, crossing his brawny arms in front of him. "I'm tempted to talk with the manager, see if I can extend her lease another month or two."

Jillian understood there was comfort in the familiar. "What would that accomplish, though?" she countered gently. "It doesn't seem like Desiree has the inclination or maybe even the ability to continue to stay here on her own."

He exhaled, looking all the more worried. "I suppose you're right about that," he conceded.

The doorbell rang. He went to get it. A forty-something woman in hospital scrubs, with kind eyes and a lively smile, stood on the doorstep. "Hi." She greeted him warmly, then looked past him to wave at Jillian and the girls. "I'm Darcy," she said as she turned back to face him. "You must be Cooper."

He shook her hand, ushering her away from the

August heat and into the air-conditioned apartment. "I am. And this is my friend, Jillian."

Friend? Jillian thought, surprised to realize that wasn't quite the label she would have wanted him to put on her. Although, she forced herself to admit realistically, what should Cooper have called her? *Former sworn enemy?*

Unaware of the tumultuous nature of her thoughts, he continued, "Desiree told me in the note she left for me that you were next door."

Darcy walked over to the girls, who were gurgling happily and waving their arms at her. She greeted and kissed each triplet sweetly, and was rewarded with even more excited chortles.

Cooper winced as Tess wiped a sticky hand on Darcy's cotton shirt, leaving a streak of partially chewed food and saliva.

The woman grinned down at her, kissed the top of her head again and then went over to the sink to take care of the stain.

Cooper remained next to Jillian, his big body coiled with tension. "Have you heard from her?" he asked Desiree's friend.

Darcy dried her hands on a paper towel, nodding. "She called me when she got to Nashville yesterday. Let me know the babies were with you, or would be, as soon as your next door neighbor, Jillian Lockhart, reached you." Darcy paused to smile at Jillian again. "Which obviously you did."

"What is Desiree doing there?" Cooper asked,

moving slightly closer to Jillian, the heat from his big body enticing and enveloping her.

"Meeting with executives and talent scouts from a major recording label." Darcy paused for the first time, looking a little stunned. "She didn't tell you that?"

Cooper shook his head, frustration radiating from his eyes. "I've texted and called, but my sister hasn't contacted me in return."

Darcy sighed, her expression as understanding as her tone. "Well, I'm not surprised. Desiree probably doesn't want to jinx it by saying anything too soon. This has been such a long time coming for her. She's written over two hundred songs, and she's got such an incredible voice, I think she should have been a star a long time ago. But maybe that will happen now that she's finally getting her work into the right hands."

Well, Jillian thought, now they knew where Desiree had gone. And why. The question was, what happened next?

Chapter Seven

"What about the triplets' father?" Cooper asked Darcy a few minutes later as he walked her out. They stood in a patch of shade on the sidewalk in front of the townhome.

Darcy worried the lanyard around her neck that carried her hospital employee identification badge.

Cooper didn't know if it was the fact she was a nurse who worked with people in crisis all the time, or just the fact she had been his sister's close friend, but she seemed to understand his need to talk. Without the kids nearby.

He didn't really think the girls had understood any of what had been said thus far. But just in case, it was better they not be within earshot.

Darcy glanced at Jillian, who was still inside supervising the kids, and turned back to Cooper. "Ron never wanted kids. Never mind triplets! He left right after they were born. Then signed away all paternal rights as part of their divorce agreement."

Cooper thought about how hard that must have been on his little sister, fiercely independent as she had always been. Wishing he had been there to help see her through it, he asked, "And Desiree was okay with that?"

She nodded, matter-of-fact. "Under the circumstances, your sister thought it was best. She didn't want her kids growing up feeling unwanted, or like they were a burden to someone. And the triplets definitely would have felt that with Ron, had he been pressured into accepting some sort of joint custody agreement, even if it was only on paper."

"Still," Cooper pointed out, his own resentment building, "the kids are legally Ron's responsibility, too. He shouldn't have just been able to walk away, even if the family court allowed it."

Darcy nodded sadly. "Desiree realized that. But she also knew that even if the court mandated that Ron take care of the kids part of the time, he wasn't going to be reliable enough to do it. She didn't want to put her kids through that, or have to worry about what was going on when they were with him, or be stuck waiting for him and not have him show up, as happens to a lot of kids of deadbeat dads. So she opted to take it all on her own, same as me." Darcy gave him a look, beseeching him to understand. "I have a similar situation with my ex-husband," she explained.

Cooper didn't understand how people could abandon their family. "I'm sorry to hear that," he said sincerely.

"Yes, well," Darcy said, sighing, "it was probably for the best, and the girls were so young, they don't remember their dad leaving, which is also good. Although sometimes they do still wish they had a father."

Cooper imagined that was so.

He still missed his own folks.

And he knew from talking to Jillian the first night at Rosehaven that she missed hers, too.

Darcy forced a smile. "I do the best I can with the help of my family and friends."

He wondered if his sister was still as resilient as she had been growing up. Or if this had, understandably, worn her down. "Has Desiree been coping well, too?"

"Yes." Darcy smiled again, her affection for his sister clear. "We had each other's backs from the time she moved in, when she was pregnant."

So why, Cooper wondered, was his sister ending her lease here when the setup was so good? Was it because she could no longer afford it? "What about child support? Does Ron help her out financially?"

Darcy hedged. "He is supposed to, of course, but he's a musician, too, although a lot less successful one, so it's kind of hit and miss. Nothing she can really count on."

Cooper wondered what the chances were that Ron would wake up, if he spoke to him personally about his responsibility to his family. And remind him in no uncertain terms that there were legal channels that Desiree could pursue to collect back due child support, whether a dad wanted to pay it or not. Seeing that as one way he could help Desiree and his nieces, he asked, "Is Ron still in the area?"

Darcy gestured haplessly. "Last Desiree heard, Ron was playing dive bars up in Alaska. But he's probably moved on. He never stays in one place for long, and he gets paid mostly in cash and tips. So... there's not necessarily a money trail to follow, since I don't think he files his taxes, either."

Great, Cooper thought grimly. Another loser.

What was it about smart, pretty girls that attracted them to duds?

Still, gratified to be learning more about what his sister had been up to, after so many years of not knowing anything at all, Cooper persisted. "So there's no one else? No ex-in-laws or new guy in her life?" Like the mystery guy who had driven her out to Rosehaven? "She's been completely on her own ever since Ron left her?"

"No helpful ex-in-laws. No new guy. She's just had me and my two teenage daughters helping her out. And she has returned the favor, cooking dinner for my girls, or helping them with their homework when I pulled a double shift in the ER." Darcy smiled. "We single moms have to stick together, you know."

Cooper was beginning to see that.

The nurse turned and headed back down the walk. "But it will be good for her and the babies to be in Laramie County with you-all, too," she called over her shoulder.

He supposed it would. If his sister ever returned from Nashville or got in touch with him, that was. "Thanks."

Darcy left to pick up her daughters from high school, and Cooper went back inside. Jillian had washed the girls' hands and faces and was letting them down to play. They toddled over to the toy-kitchen area. Tess sat down and waved a spoon in the air. Hallie handed out play dishes to her two sisters. And Sadie put plastic "groceries" in a shopping basket.

Jillian studied him with her usual compassion. "You doing okay?" she asked quietly.

Was he? In truth, Cooper couldn't really say. The last twenty-four hours had brought one bombshell after another. But there was no time to dwell on it. "Sure." He brushed off her inquiry. A flash of hurt appeared in her eyes, adding to his guilt over the mounting number of people he had let down. Desiree, and by extension, his nieces. His parents. Now Jillian, too...

To his relief, she seemed to have accepted his unwillingness to bare his soul, here and now. And was suddenly all-business once again.

"How do you want to handle the move out?" Jillian inclined her head at the letter of instruction his sister had left for them.

At last, something that required no deliberation. "Quickly and efficiently," he replied, finding refuge in the enormity of the task ahead. "'Cause I don't know about you—" he looked at her speculatively "—but I've really got to get back to Laramie by tomorrow afternoon."

Without warning, her emotions were as tightly constrained as his. "Me, too."

Already regretting having pushed her away, even for a moment, he reached for the list of instructions. "So. What do you say we divide and conquer?"

Four hours later, Darcy stopped in with her two teenage girls. They both had red hair and freckles and vivacious personalities, like their mom. "How is it going?"

"Slowly," Jillian said. *Way* too slowly.

The triplets had been too wound up to go down for a nap. It had taken Cooper a couple of hours just to find a small U-Haul truck and the packing materials they would need. Which meant they had made very little progress. Worse, Cooper had been unusually quiet, aloof. Jillian couldn't blame him. He'd been hit with a lot in a very short time and was no doubt struggling to take it all in. She knew he needed time alone. But unfortunately, with all they had to do, she couldn't really give him that.

Luckily, Darcy seemed to intuit they were overwhelmed. She wrapped her arms around her two girls' shoulders, drawing them in close. "Let us help."

"We babysit for the triplets all the time," Emma said.

"And we're not going to get to see them after this." Patty's voice quavered. "At least not very much, if at all, so…"

Emma pressed her clasped hands over her heart. "It would mean a lot to us if you would let us have this time with them," she begged.

Darcy volunteered, in a calm, practical tone, "We can feed them supper and get them ready for bed, and even have them sleep over at our place tonight."

"They stayed with us lots of times when Desiree had a gig that would keep her out late," Patty explained.

Jillian glanced at Cooper. The three toddlers had already waddled over to cling to Darcy and her two daughters. They were grinning up at the company, babbling nonsensically. Darcy, Emma and Patty smiled back just as affectionately. It was clear, Jillian noted, there was a very strong bond there. One that was loving and familial. Cooper could see it, too.

He looked at Jillian, as if seeking her opinion on the matter. She nodded, her expression saying, *It's a good idea.*

Cooper swung back around to Darcy, Emma and

Patty. "Actually," he said with a relieved sigh, "that would be of enormous help."

"Great!" Darcy said.

She made sure she had everything they needed for the triplets at her place before she, her girls and the toddlers left. Then, Jillian and Cooper got down to work.

It went much faster after that. They packed up all the girls' things except for what they would need the following morning. Then the two of them put the disassembled cribs, the changing table and the oversize rocker-glider in the small U-Haul truck.

Going back inside, they paused, deciding what to do next. "Have you contacted the charity about the donation?"

His expression didn't change in the slightest. Yet there was something in his eyes, a hint of sorrow that speared her heart. "Not yet."

She glanced at her watch, noting it was now well after 8:00 p.m. Everything would be closed. "Why not?" she asked. "If we're leaving tomorrow...were you planning to just try and drop things off?"

Before he could reply, the doorbell rang. The pizza and salad they had ordered arrived. Cooper paid the delivery person, then shut the door and carried their meal to the kitchen table. "Actually, I don't think I'm going to do that just yet."

She got out the plates and silverware. Filled two glasses with water. "How come?"

He released a breath. "I think it's premature."

As he settled at the small café table opposite her, intimacy simmered between them once again. His broad shoulders lifted in a careless shrug. "We don't know how the opportunity in Nashville will work out, or even *if* it will work out."

True, Jillian thought.

It *was* hard to make it in the music business.

But his sister also seemed to have an amazing opportunity…one she was apparently prepared to give her all to obtain. Shouldn't that count for more than what Cooper was allowing for, at least right now?

On the other hand, maybe he was just being overly protective. As a way of making up for all he hadn't done up to this point?

If that were the case, she could understand that, too.

He gave her the first piece of New York style pizza. "What we do know for a fact is that Desiree's lease is up here, and she has apparently realized she can't do this without help from family, too. And I'll provide that," he promised sincerely, while Jillian divided up the Caesar salad into two bowls. "But Desiree is still going to need dishes and furniture wherever she lands," he continued sensibly.

Jillian savored the crisp crust, spicy marinara and hot, melty cheese. It was as delicious as it looked. "But if she does end up in Nashville, which *could* happen, Cooper," she pointed out, "it won't make sense to try and ship the things she wants to donate to charity clear across the country. Because that would likely cost more than it would to simply replace them.

Which is probably why she wanted to donate them in the first place."

He shifted, his knees brushing up against hers. "I get that." With a sigh, he drew back so they were no longer touching.

"But she doesn't know yet what her future as a musician is going to hold. At least not definitively, otherwise she probably would have told us. So—" he forked up some crisp romaine and shaved parmesan "—it makes sense to me for her to have the most options possible when it comes time for her to decide what's next."

Also on point, Jillian thought. Her knees continued to tingle where they had accidentally touched his. She didn't know whether it was the fact they were both orphaned and had suffered fractures in their family as a consequence. Or the fact she had secretly lusted after him for what seemed like forever, before sharing that first white-hot kiss, that was continuing to haunt her! Or even if it was the increasing closeness they felt because they were caring for the children together.

All she knew for certain was that her emotions were in high gear. And she felt both incredibly vulnerable and incredibly safe and protected whenever she was with him like this.

And that was very confusing because she had promised herself she would not recklessly surrender her heart. Not again...

Cooper took a long thirsty drink of water. He studied Jillian over the rim of the glass.

Sensing correctly his decision not to follow Desiree's explicit instructions was still bugging her, he continued, "Storing all of my sister's belongings in my empty house may seem like an overabundance of caution to you, but it will cost her nothing. And then, no matter what happens next, she will still have everything. Which will be good if she eventually decides she wants me to help her get a place nearby, where she and the triplets can live."

But was that what Desiree really wanted? Jillian wondered.

And if not, how would she feel when she found out what Cooper had done?

Was he causing more family strife unnecessarily?

Cooper looked at her thoughtfully. "Why does this upset you?" he asked finally.

For so many reasons, Jillian thought.

Mostly, though, because it brought up a lot of her own issues.

Issues she hadn't dealt with for years.

Appetite fading, she set down her slice. Cautiously, she replied, "Because it seems like you are making decisions for your sister when she expressly told you what she wanted to do. And in my view," she said honestly, "that's wrong."

Cooper wasn't surprised Jillian had taken Desiree's side over his in this situation. If there was even a side to be taken. She had always been driven by the dictates of her heart, too.

He surveyed the flushed contours of her pretty face. Asked drolly, "Are we talking about me and my sister, or *you* now?"

She sat up straight, the action lifting the sumptuous curves of her breasts. "What do you mean?" she asked indignantly, her cheeks turning even rosier.

He leaned back in his chair. "When I first started working at your family's ranch, you were the Rebel Without a Cause."

Wincing, Jillian pulled the clip from her hair, flushed. He watched as she ran her fingers over her scalp, freeing and loosening the honey-blond waves, then let her hand fall back to her lap. Though the corners of her lips turned downward, she pushed on with her feisty response. "Look. I'm the first to admit that my romance with Chip Harcourt was ill-founded..."

Empathy roiled through him. Realizing this was his chance to find out more about her, and just as consequently evening the playing field a bit, he observed lazily, "It was more than that."

She made a face, daring him to go on.

So he did. Bringing up the memory of her dazzlingly beautiful teenage self. Stomping around. Waving her lithe arms. Tossing her waist-length hair here and there.

To the point he'd spent many a night dreaming about her. Wishing he could pursue her without fear of losing his job on her dad's ranch.

Luckily, cooler heads had prevailed. Then and now. Noting she was still watching him intently, he kicked back even farther, folding his arms behind his head, and drawled, "What I remember is that you objected to pretty much anything that wasn't your idea first." He shook his head. "The number of fiery public arguments you had with your siblings and parents back then was the talk of the bunkhouse."

She scoffed. "You expect me to believe it was really that big a deal?"

Did she really have no idea how gorgeous she was? "Oh, yeah. Of course." He tested the waters to find out. "I mean, you *were* pretty hot." He shrugged, acting as if he'd barely noticed when the opposite had been true. "So that might have had something to do with all the interest…"

"Are you saying I was disrespected?" she asked, agape.

He shook his head. All humor faded. "No one would have dared," he told her. *Not with me around. Everyone had known he would have taken the head off anyone who had tried.* "But," he went on honestly, "I think more than one of the guys had a crush on you."

She chuckled ruefully. "Just not you."

Briefly, he saw something in her eyes. Hurt? Disappointment? Curiosity? Bitter regret? He wasn't sure.

Figuring it wouldn't hurt for her to know now what had been going on with him then, he rose and carried the plates to the sink. "Of course I had a crush on you."

She followed with the rest of the dishes. "And the rest of my sisters, too, I suppose?"

Intimacy descended between them. "No," he said quietly, as serious now as her question had been. "Just you."

Jillian hitched in a breath. Then leaned back against the sink, hands braced on either side of her, her guard still up. Her mesmerizing blue eyes never left his face. "Why?" she asked, her low tone as tumultuous as her mood.

He inhaled the heady fragrance of her shampoo. "I can't say exactly." He tugged playfully on a lock of her hair. "There was just something simultaneously fiery and vulnerable about you. It made me want to keep you safe."

She splayed a hand across his chest, her fingers resting over the region of his heart. "Which you did."

And he was glad he had. Although he'd been a little sad, too, because once her flirtation with Harcourt had ended, she'd gone on to college and he'd rarely seen her during the rest of his year working at the Circle L.

She dropped her hand but made no effort to move away. "How come you didn't pursue me after that?" she asked, her gaze turbulent.

He sucked in a breath. "Well, first I would have been fired from my job at the Circle L, and I needed the money." He adjusted his stance, to ease the pressure at the front of his jeans. "And second, you were too young, and naive."

She tilted her head. "You were only twenty-one."

True. "But I'd been on my own with a sister to

look after since I'd been eighteen." He recalled how ancient he had felt. "All of that, and the other stuff that came with it, aged me."

A tentative silence fell between them. "You did look wiser than your years sometimes, back then."

He sensed a smart remark lurking. "What about now?"

Her eyes gleamed with mischief. "I think you've gone backward." She started to step past him, tossing her hair with Southern belle dramatic flair. She smirked at him over her shoulder. "Now I think I'm the one with the most life experience."

He caught her by the wrist and whirled her back to him. "You don't say." He slid one arm around her waist, used his other hand to hold hers. She swayed in his arms. Breathless. As riled up as he was.

"Coop…"

He heard the urgency, saw it in her eyes. Giving in to impulse, he lifted her wrist to his lips, kissed the delicate skin. She trembled all the more. "What do you think would have happened if you'd had a crush on me, too, back then?" he rasped, ever so slowly lowering his head to hers.

Jillian smiled. "That, cowboy, is simple." She grasped the back of his neck and pulled his head all the way down to hers. Their lips meshed. "This."

Cooper knew he'd had no business flirting with Jillian when they were both under so much stress. But he hadn't figured a little banter would end up with them putting the moves on each other. And this kiss, unlike their first, was a preliminary to just that. Her lips were sweet and soft and supple beneath his. Her slender body acquiescent.

Desire pounding through him, he wrapped his arms around her middle and tugged her closer still. Her mouth opened. Their tongues tangled. Sparks lit the air around them. And he was as lost in her as he had ever imagined he could be.

Jillian had been telling herself that her first clinch with Coop could not possibly be as tempting and erotic as she recalled it. But now, with his big, strong body engulfing hers, his tongue making a lazy foray of the inside of her mouth, she could no longer deny the sizzling chemistry between them.

He was all man and he made her feel all woman. He made her feel *alive*. Which was why she had to stop this. Now. She drew back, her breath catching in her chest.

He smiled down at her, not the least bit disturbed by the connection forging between them. "Guess I shouldn't have said past tense," he said in a low, rumbling voice. Smoothing the hair back from her face, he lifted her hand to his lips and kissed the back of it. "Because what I'm feeling right now is a lot hotter and wilder than a teenage crush."

It was, Jillian concurred wordlessly, the need for a more mature connection. The kind between consenting adults? Recklessly, she let her eyes lock with his. "I want to see where this goes, too," she murmured. She wanted to find out what they had here.

Was there really something special developing between them?

Or was it a one-off?

Either way, if they made love, their curiosity about each other would be satisfied...

They'd be able to go back to taking care of the kids without the what-if-they-had question hanging between them. They'd know...

He lifted his head. "I want you. You know that."

She could feel his hardness, and higher still, the heavy beat of his heart.

"But we don't have to go anywhere near this fast..." he told her gruffly.

"I think we do," Jillian whispered back, as need unlike anything she had ever felt coursed through her. Because who knew, really, if the chance would ever come again?

Wanting him to fill up the aching loneliness deep within her, she ran her hands across his wide shoulders, down his back, to his hips. Urging him tighter against her, compelling him to help her temporarily forget her fears and live her life fully again. She wanted him to be as ready to take a chance as she was...

He groaned as her hands swept downward. Finding the masculine heat. He shuddered in response. She moved her palms upward. Fisted her hands in his shirt and held him even closer, the warmth of her body mingling pleasurably with his. She kissed him again. Ardently, purposefully.

Aware suddenly that being a successful business-woman and a beloved aunt and sister was not going to be enough.

Not wanting to overanalyze things, she added breathlessly, "I also think…it's been a hell of a couple days, and we both need to find comfort however we can." She snuggled against him, aware it had been so long, *too* long, since she had been this close to anyone. And she needed the comfort only lovemaking could bring. She paused to look him in the eye, "It doesn't have to be anything more than a fling…"

It didn't have to be anything that would cause them any trouble…

Whatever conflict he'd been feeling was eased by her casual attitude. "Well, in that case," he drawled, his sexy grin widening as he accepted the fact they were both grown-ups who knew their own minds, "I'd be happy to oblige."

He dropped a string of hot, molten kisses across her cheek, behind her ear, on the nape of her neck, before returning to her mouth.

Determined to keep things light and sensual between them, she took him by the hand and led him up the stairs to the empty room that had once been the nursery.

She moved to the wall. Eyes turbulent, he swept his hands up and down her hips. She wrapped her arms about his neck and stood on her tiptoes, better molding her curves to his hard, muscular frame. The heat of his body mingled with hers, and it felt so good. *He* felt so good. Their tongues tangled and their breaths melded as he clasped her hips and kissed her over and over. Possessing her lips as if he meant to make her his. Holding her so close they were almost one. She arched against him, wanting and needing this so much. With every beat of her heart. He eased his hands beneath her top and found her nipples, caressing them until she moaned.

With his help, she eased off her top, shorts, panties, bra. "Your turn."

His clothes followed.

Naked, impatient, they came together once again. And kissed and kissed. They caressed each other with pent-up yearning and need, then he dropped to his knees, and his lips moved lower still. The white-hot intimacy had her arching in pleasure. Making her feel more womanly and beautiful than she ever had in her life.

Closing her eyes, she gave herself over to him fully, completely. Losing what little was left of her restraint as a soft cry and an overwhelming flood of sensation swept through her.

Still shuddering, she dropped down beside him. She knew that this hookup might be foolish and shortsighted, but she wanted to deepen the connection between them so badly. And with that decision made, the flame of desire could only be doused one way. Grinning, he followed her lead and they both stretched out on the carpeted floor. "My turn to play…" she teased. Exploring the satiny-hard curves of his pecs, and the mat of hair that arrowed downward, forming a goody trail.

He was hot, hard, *throbbing* at her touch. Her heart racing, she kissed and caressed, exploring and delighting, until everything fell away but the feel and touch and taste of him. Until there was no more holding back for either of them.

He found the condom in his wallet. Together, they rolled it on, and he brought her overtop of him. One of his hands was behind her, positioning her, the other between her thighs. And then a shiver of pure delight raced through her. She rocked against him, meeting him thrust for pleasurable thrust. They kissed again. He stroked his thumb over her flesh. And then she was flying, gone. Moments later he found the same powerful release. Together, they savored fulfillment, and the sweet, hot melting bliss.

Cooper had known it was a mistake to get drawn into Jillian's inherent emotional recklessness before they made love. But as they lay together, their bodies intimately entangled, and he felt her begin to tense and shift away from him, he wished he had taken the time to properly pursue her first.

Unfortunately, his regret did not erase what had just happened. All they could do was move forward. While hoping their premature hookup hadn't wrecked things between them.

He liked having her as his friend.

He knew his nieces did, too.

He sat up, started to speak, only to have her sit up, too, and press her fingertip to his lips. "I know there is a part of you that thinks I'm still the impetuous young girl who foolishly tried to run off with a con man. And maybe," she said as she reached for her clothes, "I do like to go with my instincts sometimes. Just do what feels right in the moment." She eased on her panties, then her bra. "Like I did when I risked everything to start my own business and nurture it to fruition." She adjusted the straps on her shoulders. "But I also understand the reality of casual relationships."

His body humming at the sight of her ravishing body, he watched her put on her shorts and top. "If you're trying to tell me you make this a habit…" Reluctantly, he began to dress, too.

"No. Of course not." She went back to find her socks and sneakers. "But I have been in a serious long-term relationship before."

This was news to him. He also realized he felt a little jealous. "When?" He finished dressing and followed her back down the stairs to the kitchen.

"College and grad school." She opened the fridge and pulled out two cold flavored waters. "I started dating a fellow botanist a few weeks in that very first semester. Tim and I studied together. That led to more socializing. Before we knew it, we were a couple, and we remained so for six years."

Funny, he hadn't ever heard about it. It seemed like that would have been news in Laramie County. "Did you ever think about getting married?" he asked gruffly.

She tossed him a beverage, then, bypassing the cozy table, took a seat on the kitchen counter. "I guess I always thought that would happen someday. But then Tim got a teaching fellowship in Oregon, and my parents had just gifted me a small business loan and a parcel of land here, so I could start my antique rose business…"

He could see why she would not have wanted to move cross-country at that point. Giving her the space she seemed to require, he took a chair. "The long-distance thing didn't work out?"

Frowning, Jillian used the hem of her top to twist off the bottle cap. "Tim didn't want to try. If it wasn't going to be convenient, he didn't want to continue. So—" she tipped her head back to take a long, thirsty drink "—he broke up with me."

Fury rose within Cooper, to think of her being hurt and humiliated that way. "Well," he said, toasting her silently, "Ted—"

"Tim." She grinned.

"—sounds like a jackass to me. He certainly didn't deserve you."

Jillian ran her fingertip idly around the rim of her drink, looking pleased he had come to her defense. "Actually," she said, looking into Cooper's eyes, "Tim probably did us both a favor. Because I think the signs that it was a relationship borne out of common interest and practicality instead of wild, passionate love were there all along." She sighed sadly and shook her head. "I just didn't want to admit he wasn't really the guy for me after all, or that I'd made a second error of the heart."

Cooper could understand that. Botched romances sucked. "Do you regret all the time you lost?" he asked curiously.

"No." Suddenly, Jillian looked wiser than her years. She continued quietly, knowingly, "Because the experience did teach me something. It made me realize that things in life don't have to be one hundred percent perfect to be valuable. Sometimes you can just take the good you can experience, in a particular situation, and be happy with that. Instead of wishing for some romantic ideal of perfection that may never come along anyway."

Still trying to figure her out, he finished his drink. "Have you dated anyone seriously since Tim?"

"Nope."

He went to the fridge and got out the package of chocolate chip cookies he had seen in there earlier. "Do you want to?" He held out the package.

Jillian took a cookie. Still holding his gaze inscrutably, she admitted, "I don't know."

Hmm. This was interesting. He took a cookie himself. "Are you okay with a no-strings relationship?" Which seemed to be what they were embarking on, given the parameters she had initially set anyway.

Jillian hesitated and for a moment he thought she wasn't going to answer, but then she let down her guard just a little bit. "I'm not really sure."

Which meant, Cooper decoded, that a replay of the mind-blowing passion they had just experienced might not be possible.

Jillian hopped down from the counter and turned away. "Since I haven't ever really tried it until just now."

That made him feel better.

Maybe in her view they did have something special, after all. Even if it was only in the beginning stages.

She kept her back to him, letting the veil of her silky hair partially obscure the flushed contours of her pretty face. "In any case, now that break time is over," she said lightly, "we better get back to packing."

"You're right." He moved beside her, figuring they could talk about this more when their emotions calmed down. Especially since they still had the packing left to do. He studied her kiss-swollen lips, wishing they could make love all over again. "Do you want to work together or apart?"

Jillian paused, then said firmly, "Together. It will go faster."

Chapter Eight

"Thanks, guys." Cooper waved as the two fellow ranchers who had helped him unload the rented truck took off for San Angelo; he had accepted their offer to return the vehicle.

He turned to Jillian, who had been pushing the babies around in their triplet stroller, which they'd brought back from Dallas, while all the activity went on, and flashed a smile that reminded her how close they all had gotten in just a few days.

King walked by her side, watching over the four females.

Jillian could see why Cooper was so attached to his yellow Lab. He was not just majestically hand-some, but sweet-natured, devoted and patiently protective. As she reached down to pet the top of his silky head, the dog looked up at her adoringly.

Cooper came back to stand beside them. His hair was tousled. Yet despite the nonstop activity of the past thirty-six hours, he was still brimming with energy.

Jillian was full of adrenaline, too.

Part of it was she couldn't stop thinking about the way they'd made love the evening before in an attempt to blow off a little steam. The rest was because she knew, even if she'd told him it could simply be a one-off fling, never to be repeated, that she still wanted him. Now more than ever.

But that wasn't part of their deal. So...

He took in the downward curve of her lips, his own expression maddeningly indecipherable. "Yeah, I know. We really do need to talk about what comes next."

She paused to let his words sink in, as always, leery of revealing too much. "What do you mean?" She'd thought they had a plan that would last until Desiree returned. Had something changed because they'd made love?

Noting the babies had all drifted off to sleep, he murmured in that gruff-tender voice she loved, "Let's get these little ones on the porch and then we can talk."

Realizing all over again what a good team they made, Jillian nodded. "Okay."

He grasped one side of the triple baby stroller. She

grasped the other, and together they lifted it onto the porch, turning the stroller so it faced the sitting area.

Taking her by the hand, Cooper guided her to sit next to him on the porch swing. Suddenly feeling a little shy and discomfited, Jillian took a shaky breath then regarded him.

Damn, but he was appealing in that rugged, all-man way. Today instead of the usual denim work shirt, well-worn jeans and boots, he was wearing olive green cargo shorts and a light gray T-shirt that clung to his powerful shoulders and chest. She was wearing a peach skort and a white cotton blouse, sneakers. And although the temperature was inching up toward the high nineties, the combination of low humidity, late-afternoon shade and the steady summer breeze made it quite comfortable.

Physically, anyway.

Emotionally she was more vulnerable than she expected to be.

Cooper smiled as King stretched out in front of them. "Initially, we hoped this was only going to be a short-term thing. Now we know it could be longer than that before Desiree returns." His brows knit together. "Which means I can't keep taking advantage of you," he said in a low, regretful voice.

Was he talking about her help with the babies, or their impromptu lovemaking? No way to tell. She bit her lip and studied the turbulence in his eyes. "I'm guessing you still haven't heard back from Desiree?"

"No." He exhaled roughly, looking frustrated again. "Have you?"

Jillian shook her head. "But then I haven't really been trying very hard to get in touch with her, since I knew that you were..." *Maybe she should start. After all, Desiree was apparently texting with her best friend, Darcy.*

He rubbed a hand over his face. Grimaced. "I doubt it would do any good," he said.

Maybe. Maybe not. Then again, perhaps what he and Desiree really needed was a peacemaker to help them.

"In any case—" he settled more comfortably beside her and draped an arm along the back of the swing "—I am going to have to figure out how to handle the situation with the triplets until she comes to get them."

She turned toward him, her bare knee brushing against his. Amazed at how right it felt to be there with him like this, she said, "I thought we had a plan."

He looked at her appreciatively; she felt an answering warmth. "Temporarily, yeah, we did," he admitted in a gruff, impatient tone, "but now we're talking a much more undefined period of time. One that could be the two to four weeks she predicted, or—" he shook his head ruefully "—knowing Desiree's unchecked ambition the way I do, possibly even longer." He paused, taking her hand in his. "I have to go back to working on my ranch. And you have a business to run, too..."

She glanced at their entwined fingers. "So we'll bring in help during the day like most families with working parents do." She winced, realizing how presumptuous that sounded. Extricating her hand from his, she moved back, doing her best to contain an embarrassed flush. Waving an airy hand, said, "You know what I mean."

The corners of his sensual lips turned upward. "Are we talking about nannies?"

She shook her head, correcting him. "Volunteers from the Laramie Multiples Club. My sister Faith is one of them. They go in to help out when a family is overwhelmed."

A mixture of relief and hope filled his expression. "You think they'd assist me?"

Jillian stood and drew a calming breath. She had to stop noticing how sensual his lips were, and fantasizing about making love with him again. They had more important things to worry about than the reckless dictates of her heart.

Knowing if they sat there together much longer, they would probably end up kissing again, she squared her shoulders. "I know the club members will be happy to help us. In fact," she said, continuing to tamp down her emotions with effort, "I'll put a call in to them right now."

Cooper sat outside with his dog and the sleeping babies, watching over all and enjoying the beauty of the summer afternoon while Jillian stepped inside her house to make some calls. Twenty minutes later she was back with very good news to report.

Figuring it was entirely possible they were getting too intimate too fast, she bypassed the chance to sit next to Cooper again and pulled up a chair to sit opposite him. Which was actually a mistake, since she now had a full view of his handsome face and rugged, masculine frame.

She turned her attention back to her notes, ignoring the low insistent quiver deep inside her. Telling herself it was simply the fact she was nervous about spending so much time with him, she kept her focus on the handwritten information and relayed calmly, "First, I assumed that, due to the ongoing construction on your home, that you and the triplets will bunk here for the time being. Second—" she cleared her throat, aware his brown eyes had never left hers "—since we still have no idea what Desiree's plans are, I asked for help for the next two weeks, minimum."

Because he looked like he was about to interrupt, she rushed to say, "They understand the fluidity of the situation—that it could easily be shorter or longer. And were still happy to help us, Monday through Friday, starting tomorrow morning."

Cooper took it all in.

Noting the tension in his shoulders was easing, Jillian again consulted her notepad. "We'll have two volunteers at nine, which they assure me is more than

sufficient for one set of triplets, and they will be able
to stay until 4:00 p.m."

Jillian looked up and saw the beginning of a smile
on Cooper's face. With equal relief, she informed
him, "I should be able to get everything I need to
get done in my greenhouses accomplished during
that time period."

He leaned forward on the swing, elbows on his
thighs, his clasped hands between his knees. "I'll
make it work for me, too," he said with quiet gratitude. "Thank you."

Jillian inhaled, glad they had made it through
this land mine. "You're welcome." She took another
breath to try to calm the skittering of her heart. "In
the meantime, I asked Faith to come over for dinner this evening."

"To help out?" He sent her an ornery grin. "Or
chaperone us?"

So he did want to make love with her again!

Trying not to feel too thrilled about that, especially since she hadn't yet decided if that would be a
wise move or not, Jillian stuffed her emotions as far
down as possible, then pushed on with equanimity.
"Actually, she wants to introduce me to her new foster baby. And," she said, rising, "she should be here
shortly. So…" She gestured vaguely, giving him tacit
permission to take off and leave the babysitting to her
and her sister. "If there is anything you want or need
to do at Rock Creek this afternoon or evening…?"

"Actually, if you've got it covered—" he sent her

a grateful glance, rising, too "—there is *a lot* I could get done."

Not sure if she was relieved or disappointed she had successfully warded off another potential kiss, Jillian stepped back, creating even more physical distance between them. Reminding herself that while it was never good to overthink things, or second guess yourself, there were still times when it was prudent to move forward a little more cautiously. "Then have at it," she said, encouraging him brightly. "Faith will be here until at least nine this evening."

Another nod, this one less easy to read. "Sounds good," he rasped.

She watched with a tinge of regret as Cooper left with King. What was it about this man that tied her up in knots? she wondered with a sigh. Was it simply his innate sexiness and physical attractiveness? The mysterious emotion she sometimes saw in his dark eyes? The incredibly feminine way he had made her feel when they'd been making love? Or something more…?

She had no clue.

Knowing the rest of the day was likely to be a nonstop marathon, however, she took the opportunity to sit on the swing and rest while the babies slept.

She did her best to concentrate on upcoming tasks and avoid thinking about their uncle. But it was nearly impossible. It seemed even when he wasn't with her, he was on her mind constantly. And maybe from here on out, she thought wistfully, aware how hopelessly smitten she already was, he always would be.

Fortunately, twenty minutes later, Faith arrived with Quinn, her new foster baby. The adorable two-month-old was hanging out in a BabyBjörn carrier attached to her chest.

"Oh, he's precious," she gushed, hand to her heart. With dark black curly hair, fair skin and deep blue eyes, he was cute enough to adorn a baby advertisement. She studied his sturdy, big boned physique admiringly. "A real bruiser, too."

Faith beamed, looking happier than Jillian had ever seen her. "I know," she agreed. "He can almost turn over already. I swear sometimes I think he's getting ready to crawl."

Because the triplets were still snoozing away, and Quinn was looking drowsy, too, they sat on the swing and sipped glasses of mint tea. "What's his story?"

Faith saddened. "His mom was apparently traveling cross country, en route to a new job in Arizona. Her car got hit by a truck. She was killed instantly. It's a miracle that Quinn survived."

And yet he looked just fine. A miracle, indeed. Jillian thought about the randomness of life and death. How easily and unexpectedly one's whole life could collapse! Aware that was what scared her about the triplets' future, too, she asked, "What about the dad?"

Faith frowned. "The authorities are trying to identify him, but apparently Annette Lantz did not list anyone on Quinn's birth certificate, and her last employer did not know, either. Of course, that's not the kind of thing an employer can legally ask, in any case."

"There was no other family?"

"No." Faith gently stroked little Quinn's back, watching tenderly as he rested his face against her chest and yawned. "None. Annette's parents died when she was seventeen, and she spent the last of her childhood in foster care. Was on her own after that."

They swayed back and forth on the swing. "So does that mean you're going to be able to adopt him?"

"That's the hope." Faith smiled as Quinn's eyes closed. She looked over at her sister. "But an extensive search for other family will have to be done first, and you know how slow those kind of things are." They paused for a moment, still swaying back and forth, absorbing that. "But in the meantime," Faith said, forcing a winsome grin, "I am his mommy, and he is my baby boy."

Just don't get too attached, Jillian wanted to say. But didn't. Because she knew that Faith's late husband, Harm, had worried about that constantly; it was why they had never tried to foster-adopt as a couple. Why Harm had wanted to simply wait until they could have a child on their own.

Curious as ever, Faith asked, "How are things with you?"

A picture of Cooper flashed in Jillian's mind. She did her best to maintain a poker face. "Good."

"Mmm-hmm." Faith elbowed her lightly. "I can tell when you're holding back. Spill."

Jillian sighed. "I think I might have a thing for Cooper Maitland."

Faith chuckled merrily. "Think or *know*?"

She flushed despite herself.

Faith sobered. "Is it going to be hard for you, living under the same roof?"

Yes and no. "He's a gentleman through and through." She took another slow sip of mint tea.

Faith's glance narrowed in sisterly concern. "That's not what I'm asking. Does he feel the same sparks that you do?"

"Um." Jillian drew another deep breath. Her secret feelings were weighing on her heart. She really had to confide in someone. It might as well be the sister to whom she was the closest. "Perhaps."

"Okay." Faith looked the year older and wiser that she was. Plus she had the benefit of being happily married for six years before she was unexpectedly widowed the previous spring. "You're admittedly attracted to Cooper, and he is apparently drawn to you, so what is the problem?"

Jillian bit her lip. Remembering just how long they had been sworn enemies before forging a necessary, temporary truce.

Of course, now that she knew him better…

And realized he wasn't the nosy spoilsport she'd originally thought…

But was instead kind and decent and sexy as all get-out…

"He's the kind of man I could fall in love with. If I were interested in that. Which, of course," she added hastily, "I'm not."

"Right." Faith scoffed. "You have absolutely no interest in husbands and babies. Which is why you're now playing house with the handsome as hell rancher next door. And sharing care of his three adorable nieces indefinitely, it seems. Because you have absolutely zero interest in that kind of life."

Put that way…

Heat crept from Jillian's chest into her face. "I *didn't*," she corrected her sister precisely.

Faith's look gentled. "But now that's changed," she noted softly.

Without warning, tears formed behind Jillian's eyes. Being with Cooper and the girls…seeing them without their mother…had inadvertently brought up all her own issues. She took another small sip to ease the tight ache in her throat. "I forgot how much a big, boisterous family could fill up your life on a day-to-day basis."

Her sister patted her arm. "And now you want it again."

Forced to confront her maternal side, Jillian gestured inanely. "Am I crazy?" she whispered, aware she could very easily get her heart broken this time, and not just her pride, as had happened at the end of her past two romantic relationships.

Cooper was perfect.

And smart.

Sexy.

Commanding and capable.

But he had told her outright, he wasn't looking for love or marriage or family.

Which meant…

He could be her undoing…

Faith reached around to give her a one-arm hug that did not squish the baby boy between them. "No, you're not crazy," she whispered comfortingly. "You're just coming awake again. And that, my dear sister, is a very good thing."

Jillian hoped so. Because whatever was happening, she was in deep.

Cooper's ranch chores took longer than expected. By the time he had all the high-protein feed blocks put out, and the pasture stock tanks refilled with water, it was nearly dark.

Luckily, Jillian had texted him a while back and told him to take as long as he needed to care for his herd.

Still, he wondered if she would be irked with him when he finally parked in front of her home. The way most women were when ranch work took up too much of his time.

The lights in the windows upstairs were dim. The downstairs was softly lit, too.

Wary of waking the triplets, he let himself in,

King at his side. Warmth flowed through him when he found Jillian sound asleep on the sofa, a notepad and pen on her lap. She looked sweet and beautiful and feminine, and it was all he could do not to wake her with a kiss.

But knowing that wasn't part of their deal—not *yet* anyway—he held his desire in check and continued observing the tender, familial scene.

On the coffee table in front of her was a line of sticky notes that read: "Put baby laundry in dryer." "Fold baby laundry!" "Tell Cooper there's a dinner plate for him in fridge." "Run dishwasher."

Aware it was the first time he'd seen her make a list of household chores—usually her item notes were related to her business—he realized she must have felt a little overwhelmed without him there to help her. Guilt rippled through him. He couldn't be like his younger sister. Just dumping the kids on someone else because it was inconvenient for him. If he was going to do this, and he was, he had to be present. No matter what it took.

Stomach growling, he eased past her. Determined to do better, he went into the kitchen to feed King and fill his water bowl.

Dinner was indeed in the fridge. Taking out a luscious-looking man-size southwestern chicken salad, he sat down to eat. It was as good as it looked. There was a slice of what appeared to be homemade apple pie, too.

Finished, he put his dishes in the dishwasher,

added soap and switched it on. Working his way through the chores Jillian hadn't gotten to, he went into the laundry room and transferred the clothes to the dryer. Quietly, he walked back to Jillian's side. And just stood there a moment, debating whether to wake her or not. Finally deciding she looked content where she was, he covered her with a light afghan, motioned King to follow him and headed upstairs.

The triplets were sleeping soundly, too. Exhausted, he went into the guest room, kicked off his boots and stretched out on top of the covers. Shut his eyes.

The next thing he knew, a high-pitched wail echoed in the air. Followed by two earsplitting other cries. His feet hit the floor. King rose, too, on full alert.

Together, they rushed across the hall. Sadie lay on her back, sobbing like the world had just ended. Hallie was sitting up in her Pack 'n Play, tears streaming down her little face, as well. And Tess was standing, hands curled around the vinyl top of the portable mesh-sided bed, looking equally despondent.

Their faces were flushed with splotches of red and white.

Jillian rushed in. "What's going on?" she gasped, looking every bit as alarmed as he felt.

"Not sure." Coop reached for Hallie and Tess and lifted them into his arms.

Jillian picked up Sadie. "Oh my gosh, she's burning up!"

"So are Hallie and Tess." Their skin felt like it was on fire. But they had all stopped wailing, now that they were being held, and were now just looking confused and miserable.

"I'm calling Gabe!" Jillian declared.

Having an older brother who was an ER doctor and infectious disease specialist was certainly a plus in this situation, Cooper thought. Their conversation was brief. Finished, Jillian turned back. "Gabe's coming over."

"Good." They needed expert help.

"In the meantime, he wants us to take their temps and document what they are, and then get them all in a lukewarm bath."

"Think your farmhouse sink will accommodate all three?"

Jillian winced. "Yeah." She warned worriedly, "But they're probably not going to like it."

She was right. The girls didn't enjoy their joint middle of the night bath. But with all three sporting temp's over 102.5, there was no choice. Letting their body temperatures go higher could bring on febrile seizures. This was the fastest way to lower them.

"Maybe if we sing to them it will help," he said.

He supported the fussing Sadie and Hallie, while Jillian held on to a weeping Tess and ran the soothing washcloth over all three.

Cooper broke out into the only song he could think

of on the spot, the Willie Nelson classic, "Mamas Don't Let Your Babies Grow Up to Be Cowboys."

As his deep voice filled the kitchen, all three babies stopped protesting and cocked their heads in interest.

He elbowed Jillian playfully, urging her to join in.

She did. Their voices blending as perfectly as their bodies once did.

Several more songs followed.

Finally, the fevers seemed to break just as a knock sounded at her front door.

They wrapped all three babies in towels and went to let Gabe in. He carried his medical bag.

"Looks like things are going better," Jillian's oldest brother observed.

True, Cooper thought in relief, since the triplets' faces were no longer as flushed and none of them were crying anymore.

Gabe opened up his medical kit and took out his stethoscope and otoscope. He gestured for Cooper and Jillian to sit on the sofa, with the babies on their laps. "Let's have a look at them."

All was silent as Gabe proceeded.

Finally, her brother had finished the pediatric exams.

Sadie and Hallie snuggled in Cooper's arms, seeming to enjoy his protection as much as he was enjoying giving it. While Tess turned away from everyone else and rested her head on Jillian's shoulder.

"Well…?" she asked, as impatient for a diagnosis as Cooper was.

Gabe frowned. "Sadie has an inflamed throat. Hallie has nasal congestion. And the lymph nodes in Tess's neck are swollen. Which leads me to believe they have contracted some kind of virus. Possibly roseola, since recently there has been a statewide outbreak of that." Seeing Cooper's and Jillian's stricken expressions, he quickly added, "But not to worry, it generally runs its course in a week or less, with just acetaminophen or ibuprofen given to help reduce fever and/or discomfort."

Jillian looked down at the baby snuggled in her arms. A sweetly maternal look on her face, she tenderly rubbed Tess's back. For a woman who professed to not want children of her own, she was sure getting into the maternal role, Cooper thought.

"I thought there was a rash with roseola," she said.

Gabe sterilized his medical equipment before returning it to the bag. "There often is, although it usually doesn't show up until the fever subsides."

It still sounded serious. "How do we treat it?" Cooper asked.

"The rash doesn't itch or hurt, so usually you don't have to do anything for it. But of course, if the rash seems to be bothering them, be sure and let their regular pediatrician know."

It was Cooper's turn to pause. "I'm not sure who that is," he said, chagrined.

Jillian's brother lifted a brow. "Do you know if they are up-to-date on all their immunizations?"

Cooper hated to admit that he didn't. "No."

"Well, you're going to need to find that out and get the name of their regular physician from your sister, so you-all will have it if any complications do occur."

"I'll text her," Cooper promised.

As unfortunate as this was for the triplets, maybe this was the reality check his sister needed. To start fully living up to her obligations as a mother.

Jillian accepted the two small bottles of child acetaminophen and ibuprofen her brother gave her. "Is it contagious? Because," she said, worried, "Faith was here this evening with Quinn…"

Her brother held up a hand, staving off her concern. "Usually, babies are immune from roseola until they reach six months of age. But I'll talk to her and tell her what to watch out for in any case. Needless to say, she and Quinn shouldn't be here again for about a week, when the triplets are no longer contagious. Or anyone else who would be susceptible, either."

Cooper nodded. "Right."

Gabe closed his medical bag and headed for the door. Jillian followed him to the portal. Hands full of sleepy baby, she gave him a familial kiss on his cheek. "Thank you so much for coming, big brother."

Unable to shake his hand with his arms full of babies, Cooper sent the former Physicians Without

Borders doc a grateful look. "We really appreciate it," he added.

"No problem. Let me know if there is anything else I can do." Gabe departed.

Cooper and Jillian spent the next half an hour diapering and dressing the babies in clean dry clothes and giving them bottles of chilled apple juice and water.

By then, they were sleepy.

Cooper carried their Pack 'n Plays downstairs, and they settled them in with their blankets and teddies. Minutes later, all were fast asleep.

It was 5:00 a.m. Cooper felt like he'd just run a marathon. Jillian looked like she was completely drained, too. "Well, so much for the big plans we had for today," she said.

Cooper sighed. Because she looked as if she needed a hug as much as he did at that moment, he drew her into his arms. Briefly rested his face in the silky hair on the top of her head. "Priorities, right?" he murmured.

Jillian clung to him for a moment, then drew back. She had that look on her face again. The one that said she wanted to leap into a full-blown affair with him. But wouldn't. She eased away from him, gathering up the damp towels left over from the kids' fever-reducing baths, then headed for the laundry room. "The kids have to come first." She tossed the words over her shoulder. "Everything else will be secondary."

Although it didn't make him want her any less, Cooper agreed. "Speaking of which…" He reached for his phone. Then added soberly, "Maybe it's time I notify Desiree that her babies are sick."

Chapter Nine

Jillian and Cooper decided to use the opportunity presented to shower and get dressed for the day. She went first, and while he was upstairs and the triplets were still sleeping, she whipped up some breakfast for both of them.

"Something smells good." He stood in the doorway, dressed in a light gray T-shirt and worn jeans. Her eyes drifted over him. Cooper's dark brown hair was still damp and smelling of shampoo, his face cleanly shaven. As he neared her, she caught the faint minty fragrance of his toothpaste and the more masculine smell of his soap.

A thrill swept through her.

Pretending a casual ease she couldn't begin to feel,

she turned away and began crumbling fried tortilla strips and cheddar and Monterey Jack cheeses into the scrambling eggs in the pan. Gave them a stir. "Migas."

He ambled nearer, taking in the bowl of chopped tomato, onion, jalapeño, cilantro and lime juice. "You made pico de gallo, too?"

She basked beneath his praise. "Of course." Realizing what a pleasure he was to cook for, she set a platter of crisp bacon on the table, along with a full carafe of freshly brewed coffee. Then turned the eggs into a serving bowl. "Any word from Desiree yet?"

His phone pinged. They both tensed. "Well, actually, to my amazement, yes..." he murmured.

He motioned her closer. She stood, so she could see his phone. A message appeared on the screen.

Triplets up to date on all immunizations. Medical records with West Dallas Pediatric Group. A phone number followed, with a link to the medical practice's website. Docs there should be able to tell you whatever you need to know.

Cooper's tall body sagged in relief. Thanks, he texted back. When will you be home?

Bubbles appeared on screen that indicated the other person was typing, then abruptly stopped.

Jillian froze, and he swore beneath his breath.

Then the bubbles started again. Stopped. Started. Finally, a new message appeared.

Cooper, I know you don't understand. The truth is, you never did. But I have to focus here. We'll talk when we see each other again.

Frowning, he typed back, And when will that be exactly?

Nothing.

He waited. Waited some more. Then finally put the phone down and turned it over so he could no longer see the screen.

Able to see how disappointed he was, Jillian sat opposite him. They filled their plates and began to eat. She felt compelled to offer some comfort. "It's still pretty early. Barely six a.m."

Cooper nodded, his expression closed.

She swallowed. The breakfast she had taken such care to make now tasted like sawdust in her mouth. "Desiree may have just woken up…"

Cooper put down his fork, then sat back. "Why are you making excuses for her?" he growled.

Beginning to see for herself how complicated and demanding motherhood was, never mind for a woman trying to do it all on her own, Jillian turned her hands, palm up. "Because I'm trying to give her the benefit of the doubt."

"And…?" he prodded, sensing there was more.

Jillian sighed and picked up her fork again. "I don't want to see the two of you fighting."

To his credit, Cooper didn't appear to want that, either. It didn't mean he wasn't still worried and disappointed. Finally, he swallowed and shook his head. "Here's what I don't get." He paused to look Jillian in the eye. "Desiree's babies are all sick." He paused, in that moment, looking as heartbroken and disillusioned as Jillian felt. "And she's apparently not even going to bother to come home to care for them?"

Jillian thought about the way she and Cooper had both raced to the children's aid at the first sound of trouble, and knew nothing would keep them from rushing to the rescue once again.

So, in that sense, Desiree's behavior baffled her, too.

On the other hand, she didn't know all or even most of the facts of the situation. Nor was it right for her to judge.

The only person who had walked a mile in Desiree's shoes was Desiree...

Jillian sipped her coffee, which had grown lukewarm. And struggled to be empathetic. "She trusts you to take care of them."

Grooves etched on either side of his beautiful mouth, Cooper nodded. He finished his breakfast, and after noticing that King was also done with his meal, he took his plate and utensils to the dishwasher and slid them inside. Then he grabbed his coffee cup, topped it off and signaled for the dog to follow him outside. "Or she just doesn't care." He tossed the terse words over one broad shoulder.

He and King walked past the girls, who were still sleeping soundly in the living room, and eased out onto the porch.

Figuring he needed a sounding board, Jillian walked outside, too. The dawn sky was streaked with pink, gray and blue. And the morning air was warm and humid. She sat on the swing, her mug cupped between her palms, and watched him pace back and forth. Playing the part of devil's advocate, she pointed out calmly, "Everything we've seen about the girls to date, their general state of happiness and well-being, says your sister does care about her baby girls."

Cooper swung back toward her, his nostrils flaring slightly. "Then why in the hell did she walk out on them?"

Was that what Desiree had done? In Cooper's view, yes. Maybe not in Desiree's. "She went to Nashville because she had the opportunity to provide a better life for them."

A muscle ticked in his jaw. "If everything works out," he stated.

Jillian put the toe of her shoe down and stopped the swing from swaying back and forth. "Why are you so sure it won't?"

His expression clouded over. "Because she's a lot like our mom."

This was news. Jillian shifted over to make room for him. "She was a singer-songwriter, too?"

"No." Cooper exhaled, and came back to sink down beside her. He reached over and took her hand in his, idly stroking the back of it. "An entrepreneur."

Tingles swept through Jillian. Followed swiftly by the heat of need.

"Or at least she really wanted to be," Cooper continued, tightening his grip on her fingers.

"How so?" Jillian asked quietly, when he didn't go on.

He shook his head, recalling, "The whole time we were growing up, my mother was incubating some small business idea or another." Sighing, he sat back. "Everything from a monogram sewing business to a pet-sitting service to furniture reupholstering and refinishing."

Jillian could see Cooper was unhappy about his mother's efforts; she didn't know why. "Did the businesses fail?"

Another shake of his head. "Actually, they were all really successful, on a small scale."

Well, that was good, she thought.

"But none of them were the kind of thing she was able to franchise, and that was what she wanted. So she sold them—usually for not much more than what she put into them—and moved on to the next big thing."

Which had no doubt put financial stress on the family, Jillian surmised. Wondering if that was the reason behind Cooper's disgruntlement, she asked, "What about your dad? Was he partners with her?"

"No." Cooper turned toward her and cupped both her hands in his. "He was a high school science teacher and a cross-country track coach. A one step at a time kind of guy who believed it's the turtle not the rabbit who always wins the race."

Jillian's pulse raced at his touch. "So in other words, you are more like he was."

"I guess." For a moment something flickered in his expression, disappeared. "Yeah."

Briefly, they sat in contemplative silence. As always, his ultramasculine presence made her feel acutely aware of him. Determined not to think about how much she longed to pull him close and kiss and make love to him again, she went back to the subject at hand. "Yet your dad and your mom hit it off?" As in opposites attract?

Cooper smiled, reflecting contentedly. "They had a great marriage. Always supported each other." A shadow crossed his face. "In fact, it was because he was so determined to be there for her that they went on that last trip that cost them their lives."

Jillian blinked. Watching him stand and begin to pace once again. This time, she followed him. "I don't understand."

Cooper lounged against one of the pillars that supported the porch roof. "My mom had decided a food truck was where it was at. This was at the very beginning of the craze. The cost of owning one, however, was prohibitive."

She knew, from watching a TV program on them, that they could easily run upward of several hundred thousand dollars.

Cooper's brows drew together. "But she finally

found one that she and dad felt they could fix up. They were on their way to Abilene to purchase it when a freak storm hit, and their pickup got washed off a low water crossing and swept into the river."

Jillian gasped.

"It flipped over on its roof." Soul-deep sorrow laced his voice. "They both drowned before they could get out."

"Oh, Cooper, I'm so sorry." Her heart going out to him, she took his hand.

He accepted her comfort with the tenderness in which it was given, then wrapped his arms around her shoulders and enveloped her in a big hug. "I know you and your siblings understand what it's like to be on the receiving end of sudden, horrific tragedy."

Jillian thought back to the house fire and resulting explosion that had taken her parents, which had also been the result of a horrible storm.

He tensed in silent admonition. Let her go and stepped back. "The last thing my parents said to me before they left was, 'Coop, take care of your sister,'" he recounted bitterly, folding his arms. "I promised that I would."

She felt strangely bereft now that he'd pulled away, but because he seemed to need his physical space, she let him have it. Remaining where she stood with difficulty. "And you did that for them, for her, for three years, Coop."

He sighed, and seeing King was finished in the nearby field, signaled for his pet to come back onto the porch and inside the house. Then after checking on the sleeping girls, he went back to the kitchen. His phone was still facedown on the table. He turned it over.

Jillian was disappointed to see nothing new.

Misery etched the handsome lines of his face. "Apparently, I didn't do well enough. Not then. Not now," he countered somberly. "Otherwise—" his hurt reverberated between them "—she would at least pick up the phone when I called."

Jillian could not bear to see him so miserable. Especially when he did not need to be!

Taking him by the wrist, she drew him into the adjacent laundry room and shut the door behind them to keep their voices from carrying and prematurely waking the girls.

"Listen to me, Coop," she said. "I know it's hard. But you cannot live in the past." She splayed her hands across his chest, imploring him to listen to her. "You have to focus on the here and now."

His mouth set grimly. He looked torn. "I have to think about the future, too."

"No…you don't! Not now. Not today."

And to prove it, she kissed him.

It wasn't the first time Jillian had used passion as a panacea. Or the only instance he had accepted comfort from her in this way. But it *was* the first time he set aside all gentlemanly instincts, threaded his hands through her hair, and without a single reservation, met her kiss for aching kiss.

She surged against him wildly, pressing her breasts against his chest and running her hands up and down his spine. A rush of need coursed through him and the anger, regret and frustration he had been feeling for days now finally began to ease.

This was what he needed, he thought, as she rocked against him restlessly, her pliant body surrendering all the more. *She* was what he needed. And damn it all, if she didn't seem to realize it, too, he thought in wonderment.

"Coop," she whispered, her slender body melding into his. "Make love with me now. Please."

He could hardly refuse her.

Still kissing her, he lifted her, positioning her legs around his waist. "Your wish is my command, darlin'."

Quietly, they moved through the downstairs and up to the second floor. Her bedcovers were still rumpled. The room smelled of roses, just as her hair and skin did.

He set her down beside the bed. Dropped his head, and kissed her slow and wet, hard and deep. He was in no hurry, slowly and sweetly taking his time feasting on her lips. Until she moved impatiently against him…wanting more.

She stepped out of her shoes. Reached for his shirt, tugging it over his head.

With a husky laugh, he slipped off her T-shirt

and bra, unsnapped her shorts and eased her panties down her thighs. Her hands rested on his shoulders, while he helped her step out.

"You're so beautiful," he whispered. "So smokin' hot."

Grinning back at him, she eased off his jeans and drew down his boxer briefs. "Right back at you, cowboy." Her palms stroked him in an ever-widening circle. His body hardened. He knew he would never make it if he let her have full rein.

His thumbs caressed the curves of her breasts, gently caressed her nipples. Savoring the sight of her, he drew her over to sit on the side of the bed. Easing her knees open, he knelt between them. He traced her with his fingertips and kissed her again, until she clung to him like a lifeline. Aware even as he found her, *there*, with his lips and tongue, that she was on the brink. And then she was gone, clutching his head, shuddering at the tender intimacy of their connection. And he was nearly gone, too.

"Coop…" she murmured again. Impatient, wanton, now.

Heart pounding in his chest, he exited just long enough to retrieve a condom. She lay back against the pillows, watching, mesmerized, as he rolled it on. And then they were together, kissing again. He was stretched out overtop of her. Her legs wrapped around his hips.

She was wet and open.

He was hot and hard.

And then there was no more waiting. He gave her what she wanted and needed. Filling and stretching. Thrusting into her over and over again. Feeling her arch up against him and hold him close. So close...

Soon they were both groaning for more. Climbing toward the summit. Moving way too fast and hitting the pinnacle at exactly the same time.

Afterward, they clung together, breathing hard. Coming slowly, blissfully down. Aware he had never felt satisfaction like this, he rolled onto his back, bringing her with him as she inundated him with her sweet, sultry softness. Her body still quivering with aftershocks, she slumped against him. Making no effort to quickly ease away this time.

At least not yet.

Emotions soaring, he stroked a hand through her hair. Glad they had made love again. And this time, weren't running from the consequences afterward. Wondering if she was ready to take their relationship a little further into the future, he kissed her temple, then murmured lightly, "So, darlin'. Does this mean our hookup isn't a one-off after all?"

Jillian hadn't expected any of this. But she couldn't fight it, either, not when the two of them were residing in such close quarters. Because the absolute truth was, his every touch, every kiss, sent her spinning.

He made her feel more of a woman than she ever had in her life. And she wanted him, in her arms, in her bed, in her life. She wanted him to end the aching loneliness inside her and help her live again—*really* live. The way her parents and happily married siblings did.

Even if it was only for a while.

And if this was the way it happened—spontaneously—then so be it, she decided. Especially when they both had geysers of emotion roaring within them right now.

She rolled onto her side and propped her head on her hand. Noting with pleasure that he looked sexier than ever, after they made love. She traced the width of his shoulders with the flat of her palm, loving the satiny feel of his skin. "I admit initially I thought one roll in the hay might satisfy our curiosity and end the attraction."

Mischief danced in his sable eyes. He scored the pad of his thumb playfully across her lower lip. "And now?"

"I'm guessing," she drawled, tossing her head flirtatiously and releasing a lusty sigh, "probably not."

His laughter echoed the joy she felt bubbling up inside her. "So what are we going to do about that?" he asked, grinning with masculine satisfaction.

She sat up, dragging the sheet over her breasts. Forced herself to look into his eyes and say what was on her mind. "Agree to be friends-with-benefits," she proposed.

Disappointment briefly crossed his face, then disappeared. "For how long?" he asked casually.

She drew another tumultuous breath. Not wanting to scare him off or wish for too much, she chose her words carefully. "For as long as the situation works," she answered.

He kissed the back of her hand and replied gruffly, "Sounds good to me."

Chapter Ten

"Sounds like you've had quite the week and a half," Carol Lockhart said to Jillian when she stopped by, tan and rested from her Hawaiian vacation.

Jillian looked over at the triplets, who were playing with the faux kitchen set they'd brought from their Dallas home, now set up in a corner of Jillian's living room.

Their rashes were gone, and they had been fever-free for a good forty-eight hours, which meant they were no longer contagious.

Pleased, Carol continued, "You seem to be handling them well."

In truth, it was a surprise to Jillian, too. She'd always considered herself a great aunt. But there was a big difference from being a loving relative who swooped in and out, "bringing the fun" and delivering hugs and kisses, and stepping into the full-time shoes of a "mom." Being a parent required the kind of intuitive multi-tasking skills she hadn't really been sure she possessed. Until now.

After the past few days, she knew she was not just up to the challenge of caring for multiple children 24/7, but that she wanted to do it. Not just because she was pretty darn good at it, after all, but because loving the triplets and tapping into her maternal side made her life so much richer.

Of course she'd had Cooper to help her.

And sharing the responsibility had brought them a heck of a lot closer, too. Both in tangible and intangible ways.

Jillian handed her mother a fresh cup of coffee, laced with half-and-half. And sat down in the extrawide rocking chair that had come from Desiree's apartment. Forcing herself to admit she wasn't Superwoman, even though she sometimes felt like it these days, she said, "They are actually pretty easygoing babies. When they're not sick."

Carol settled on the sofa. "I imagine they were pretty fussy the first few days…"

Jillian shook her head. Letting her mother know that had not been the case.

"Not at all?" Carol asked in surprise.

"Well, of course, they were fussy when they were

sick. But Cooper is *really* good with them." He had a way of soothing them that was almost magical.

Again, her mom looked surprised.

"He sings to them," Jillian explained.

"Lullabies?"

Jillian flushed and went back to the kitchen to get a fresh cup of coffee for herself. She ducked her head as she stirred in the vanilla creamer. "Ah. I'm not sure he knows any of those…"

Carol smiled. "Then what does he sing?"

Feeling a little like she was a teenager who had just come in late from a date and was facing parental inquisition, Jillian took her time coming back to the living area. She smoothed the hem of her cotton skirt as she sat kitty-corner from her mom once again. Abruptly aware that since Cooper had temporarily "moved in" she was dressing a little better. And taking more care with her hair and makeup. To her discomfort, her mom had noticed, too.

"What kind of songs, then?" Carol persisted, curious. "If not lullabies?"

Back to Cooper. As if she didn't think about him enough already! Or secretly wish that the two of them were already moving on from their agreed upon Friends with Benefits agreement to something more lasting that included love. And in her wildest dream of all, maybe even starting a family of their own!

But knowing no one else needed to know that, especially her mom, Jillian did her best to maintain a poker face, and sipped her hot and delicious flavored coffee. Seeing from her mother's quirked brow that Carol was not going to let this line of questioning go, she really wanted to know what it was Cooper sung, she sighed and put down her mug. "If you must know, Mom," and she really didn't see why it was necessary! "Cooper belts out country-western standards."

Her mom smiled again, as if trying to picture that. "Like…?"

"'Friends in Low Places.'" Jillian rotely recited the most frequent. "'Diamonds Make Babies.'" *Whoops. She shouldn't have said that.*

In vain, she tried to think of another.

But all she could think about now was the last time she had made hot, wonderful, wild and tender love with Cooper.

And how afterward, she couldn't help but wish that one day when this was all over, and Desiree was back, maybe she and Cooper would consider having a family of their own. Even if it was in an untraditional, non-married sense.

After all, she knew plenty of people, including her own sister Mackenzie and her now-husband, Griff, who had started out as friends with a baby or babies on the way, who were now madly in love with each other and happily ensconced in a forever kind of family.

That could happen to her and Cooper, too. Couldn't it? And if it didn't, she could still have a baby on her own…

Or foster-adopt, like Faith.

Fortunately, Carol was ready to move on. "When is his sister coming back?"

Another tough subject. She traced the handle of her mug with her index finger. "We don't know exactly."

"Roughly, then." Her mom beamed as Sadie toddled over to give her some plastic groceries. "Thank you, sweetheart," she said.

Sadie flashed a toothy grin and toddled off to her sisters.

Aware her mom was still waiting to hear the timetable, Jillian shrugged. Then took her best guess. "Probably in another week or two. Or three…"

Her mom sobered. "Have you been in touch with her?"

Another sticky question. "She has texted Coop. About their medical records." Not before or since.

"But not called?" Carol smiled as Tess came over to hand her a stuffed animal. The gift warranted a hug of thanks, and then Tess toddled back to the play kitchen.

Carol turned back to her daughter, waiting.

Once again, Jillian found herself coming to the defense of Cooper's sister. "I think Desiree's pretty busy in Nashville, with the folks at the record company."

Carol took another sip of her coffee. "What about your antique rose business?"

Ah! Something that in theory anyway should have been a lot easier to discuss. "There is no question

I am behind on shipping product," Jillian admitted reluctantly.

From Carol's expression, her mother had expected as much. "And the greenhouses?"

"I had help making sure the plants were cared for." And that wasn't surprising, since Laramie was a place where neighbors helped neighbors. Once the word had gotten out about the triplets' roseola, landscapers and horticulturalists from all over the county had arrived to pitch in. Most volunteering for an hour or two. But that had been enough.

"What about Cooper?"

"He's had friends helping over at Rock Creek. Making sure his cattle are okay. His dog, King, has been here with him." Until Cooper had found out her mom had planned to come by. Then, he had graciously offered to make himself and King scarce. And she had reluctantly agreed it was probably for the best.

Her mom went into the kitchen to top off her mug. She also stirred in more half-and-half. "Where is he now?"

"At his ranch."

"I see." Carol studied her from over the counter. "When do you plan to go back to work?"

"This afternoon. We have volunteers from the Laramie Multiples Club coming to help out with the triplets. So we will both be taking care of our businesses then."

Her mom returned to her side. "I guess you and Cooper are getting along well, then?"

An understatement if there ever was one. In fact, had the situation been different, Jillian would have considered dropping her guard entirely and pursuing him romantically. For keeps. But with things already getting way too complicated, she knew it wasn't a good idea to go down that road. Not yet, anyway.

Candidly, she told her mom, "We make a pretty good team when it comes to caring for the girls." An even better one when it came to satisfying each other's physical needs. Not that she planned to divulge that to her mother!

Carol nodded as Hallie toddled over and climbed onto the older woman's lap for a cuddle. "Well, I think your sacrifice in this case has been admirable." She gently stroked Hallie's curls.

"Thanks."

"But…" she said, sighing contentedly as Hallie leaned back to cuddle all the more, "you don't have to do this all yourself."

Jillian quirked an eyebrow. "What do you mean?"

"Well," Carol suggested practically, "now your dad and I are back. Our house is a whole lot bigger. We would be happy to host Cooper and his nieces for the time being."

What? Jillian straightened. She had not seen this coming! "I don't think he would want to do that," she told her mother stiffly.

"Why not?"

Because it would mean she and Cooper would not be spending any more time together. Not like they were now, anyway. Doing her best to keep her escalating emotions under wraps, Jillian focused on what she could discuss. "The girls are settled in here, and because my home is a lot smaller, it's a lot easier to watch over them. I mean, if it's not broke, why fix it?"

"Because," Carol said gently, like the veteran social worker she was, "a situation like this can breed a false intimacy. One that usually ends as abruptly as it started when the situation comes to a close." She radiated empathy and concern. "I don't want to see you get hurt."

Jillian watched Hallie climb down from her mom's lap and return to play with her sisters. "Why would you think that could be the case?" Unable to help herself, she added defensively, "Why would you think Cooper would ever hurt me?"

Her mother waved an airy hand. "Because of the way you light up whenever you say Cooper's name. Unless…there is something else going on here, too, apart from your enforced proximity? Something *romantic*?" she suggested.

Heat climbed from her chest into her face. "Mom, really!"

"Not an answer, Jillian."

"And you're not going to get one," she huffed. Suddenly she felt the way she had when she was a kid, trying to date con man Chip Harcourt over her parents' express disapproval.

Her mother sighed and sent a glance heavenward. "I'm *not* trying to upset you, honey."

"Really?" Jillian stormed back into the kitchen and set her mug in the sink. "Because you're doing a very good job of it!"

Her mom followed with the patience of a saint. "Just know that your dad and I are here for you," she said steadily. "For whatever you need, *whenever* you need it. And that goes for Cooper and his nieces and his sister, too."

Guilt flooded through her. "I know that, Mom," she murmured, a little embarrassed at how she had overreacted, and in the process likely given away her secret crush on Cooper.

More understanding than ever, Carol hugged her affectionately. Then pulled away and smiled. "Now, on to more pressing matters…" she said.

Hours later, Cooper returned to find Jillian and his three nieces dressed in their Sunday best. It didn't take him long to find out why.

"We're having dinner with your entire family? *Tonight?*" he repeated, stunned. Aware that unlike the four gals, he was covered in the grime associated with a long day of working cattle and repairing things around the Rock Creek ranch.

Jillian found her phone and SUV keys and tucked both into her handbag. She'd put her hair up in some sort of loose, sexy twist, and looked absolutely gorgeous in a pretty floral print sundress. It had a fitted bodice and wide straps that showed off her toned and sexy upper half, before dropping in a swirl of fabric to her knees, and doing similar things for her satiny smooth calves.

In that instant he realized he had been taking her for granted. Probably not paying enough attention to his own grooming and attire. But no more.

He was going to make sure she got what she deserved.

She swung back to him, inundating him with a drift of her signature rose fragrance. Mistaking his silence for some sort of objection, she paused, then said, "Well, the girls and I are having dinner with my entire family. If it's okay with you, of course. You don't have to go," she explained, a hint of disappointment in her expression, "but you were invited, too."

He ran a hand over his stubbled jaw. Clearly he was going to have to shave and shower and change. He took off his dusty boots and left them by the door. "I'm surprised your folks want to host a big gathering since they just got back from Hawaii," he said.

"Actually…" Jillian removed bottles of formula from the fridge and half a dozen jars of baby food from the cupboard, then stuffed them all into the carryall, next to the diapers.

She bent to pick up three pairs of baby shoes, giving him a great view of her delectable derriere. Completely oblivious to the effect she was having on him, she spoke over her shoulder. "Mom and Dad got back late the night before last and took all of yesterday to rest up and adjust from the time change. Anyway…" Jillian glided past him.

Still mesmerized, he watched as she settled on the sofa and coaxed the girls onto her lap, one at a time, to get their footwear on.

"My mom stopped by this morning and told me that my brother Noah's girls are still having a hard time adjusting to the move to Laramie."

Cooper wasn't surprised. First, they'd lost their mom to cancer and then they'd had to leave the only home they'd ever known in California. It was a lot for Noah's eight-year-old and preschooler twins to handle.

"Mom thought it might help their spirits if we got everyone together. Because the only thing Noah's daughters like better than cousins and animals are babies." She snuggled the triplets affectionately. Grinning as they climbed all over her and snuggled her right back. "And these little gals are cute as can be."

They sure were, Cooper thought. Especially all dressed up in frilly dresses, with little satin bows in their hair.

Not wanting to miss out on what sounded like a fun evening, he asked, "Can you give me ten minutes to get cleaned up?"

Her face lit up. "Sure. I need to do a few last minute things, anyway."

When Cooper returned, the girls were still snuggled around Jillian, listening to her read a Sandra Boynton book. They made such a heartwarming picture, he felt his chest expand with love.

He realized he was really going to miss them when this time together came to an end. His days and nights were never going to be the same.

"You're awfully quiet," Jillian said on the fifteen-minute drive to the Circle L Ranch.

They were taking her SUV. But she had offered him the keys. Cooper tightened his grip on the steering wheel. Aware that a downside to partaking in the Lockhart family dinner was that there would likely be a lot of questions he had no way to effectively answer.

He reached across the console to touch her arm. Squeezed it lightly, affectionately, admitting gruffly, "I'm just wishing I knew when Desiree would be back."

Jillian cast a fond look at the girls, snug in their car seats. "As soon as she can, I am sure."

And what then? Cooper wondered. Would Desiree want to take off again? Have the girls with her? Or leave them behind?

There was no way to know.

Luckily, there was no more time to discuss it, since her parents' ranch came into view. It had expanded even more since he had worked there for a year in his twenties. Impeccably maintained split-rail fences still lined the long drive up to the main house.

A dozen cars and trucks crowded the circular drive located in front of the sprawling two-story white stone ranch house. The handsome Craftsman-style front door, cedar shutters and light charcoal roof all added to the rustic farmhouse vibe that perfectly suited the ten-thousand-acre cattle ranch.

As they got out, they were surrounded by Jillian's three sisters, four brothers and an assortment of nieces and nephews.

"We want to see the babies!" Noah's three-year-old twin daughters announced, while his oldest child hung back, a scowl on her face.

Gabe and Susannah's six-year-old quintuplets stopped playing soccer long enough to join in.

Meanwhile, Cade and Allison's eighteen-month-old twins watched from the stroller they were riding in, and Faith snuggled her new foster son, Quinn, in a BabyBjörn carrier. Mackenzie and her husband Griff were using baby carriers for their nine-month-old twin infants, too.

It was definitely a kiddie bonanza, Cooper observed. He couldn't help but note Jillian looked enthused and excited to be part of it.

Short minutes later, all the little ones were ensconced in the massive air-conditioned family room, with some of the women watching over them, others working in the kitchen on the other side of the space.

Robert Lockhart and his son, Travis, the only offspring to choose cattle ranching as a career, were still out at the barn, checking on the new heifers Robert had picked up at auction.

Cooper was about to head down that way himself when Jillian's brother Cade intercepted him.

"Hey," the former professional pitcher said, "want to help set up the grills?"

"Sure." Cooper fell into step beside him.

Cade walked through the garage to the shelves where the outdoor cooking gear was stowed. "Gabe's manning the gas grill. Griff is overseeing the smoker. You and I have the charcoal grill."

He nodded, impressed. "A lot of cookers going."

Cade handed Cooper a big bag of charcoal. Then picked up two large metal chimneys and a lighter. Grinning, he led the way onto the back patio. "A lot of mouths to feed when all the Lockharts get together these days."

"True."

The other man stopped in front of a long rectangular grill. "And this way we can all take home a few leftovers."

Easily able to see the advantage in that, Cooper lifted the rounded lid and set it on its hinges. "Even better."

Cade ripped open the bag and Cooper tipped the open end into the openings of the metal charcoal starters. When they were filled to the brim, he removed the cooking grates. Then Cade put the charcoal chimneys in the bottom of the grill and lit the coals inside. Fragrant smoke curled upward.

They settled in a couple of nearby chairs while they waited. "Heard your sister is up for some big deal in Nashville," Cade remarked eventually.

"Yeah."

Cade exhaled. "Well, I hope it all works out."

Aware the former pro athlete understood better than anyone that stardom could be fleeting, Cooper grimaced.

"Me, too," he said honestly.

"Lucky that Jillian was around to help you out with the triplets."

Yep, Jillian's family was definitely checking out his intentions. Not that he blamed them. If he had been in their place, he would have been protective, too.

Cooper bobbed his head in agreement. He looked Cade in the eye and stated sincerely, "I'm grateful for her help. That's for sure." *Had he actually come out and told Jillian that? Maybe not...*

He definitely should.

Cade got up to check the flames licking out the top of the charcoal chimney. Satisfied all was as it should be, he sat back down. "She owes you, too, even if she may not exactly realize it yet."

"For what?" Cooper asked, curious.

Cade grinned. "Helping my sister realize how much she really does want and need a family...kids... of her own."

Cooper paused. "Did she say that to you?"

The other man shook his head, explaining candidly, "Didn't have to. I saw it on her face the minute you-all got out of the SUV with the babies. And of course it was evident in her many phone conversations with Allison this week when they were trading 'parenting tips' and talking about 'new mom' stuff."

Cooper remembered the frequent chats. He'd just assumed Jillian was searching for information and hadn't attached any emotional importance to it. Too late, he saw he should have.

Cade kicked back in his chair, reflecting, "It's not going to be enough for Jillian to simply be a single aunt after this." He shook his head in fond observation. "She won't be content until she has it all. That special person to walk through life with. Marriage. Kids. The whole shebang."

All the things Jillian had sworn for years she did not want or need...

Cade slapped Cooper on the shoulder, finishing with brotherly approval, "And her sea change is all thanks to you..."

Chapter Eleven

"It's a good thing we put Sadie, Tess and Hallie in their pajamas before we left my folks' ranch," Jillian whispered hours later as they backed out of the temporary nursery in her home.

All three girls were now snoozing contentedly, their blankets and teddy bears beside them.

Cooper couldn't help but smile at the sleeping trio. They looked so sweet and innocent. Not knowing that their actual mom had showed very little interest in them over the past week and a half.

And might not, he was beginning to fear, ever come back.

Of course they would have him.

And Jillian.

But would it be enough?

Was it fair of him to even ask her to take on such a life-altering task?

Particularly when her brother Cade had pointed out that he thought she had finally come to the conclusion that she wanted kids of her own?

Blissfully unaware of his private worries, Jillian headed back down the stairs, her mood as buoyant as it had been all evening. When she reached the foyer, she gave him a flirtatious look. "I don't suppose I could interest you in helping me bring those boxes in from my SUV?"

He had been wondering about those. The Lockhart women had carried them out to her vehicle and stowed them in the back just as they were leaving. She had yet to tell him what that was all about.

Amazed at how fresh and pretty she could look after an evening spent chasing after toddlers, helping out in the kitchen and trading lively stories with her siblings, he offered, "I'll do it for you."

She winked. "I'll help."

Together, they went out to her Tahoe. Three opaque plastic storage boxes with lids were lined up side by side. He carried two. She took the last.

"I can't wait to go through this stuff." She shifted a box to her hip and held the door for him.

He studied the chain-hung silver heart nestled in the soft valley just above her breasts. "What is it?"

She tilted her head, and the gentle movement

brought the subtle drift of her perfume. "Lockhart family hand-me-downs."

He smiled and locked eyes with her. "For you?"

She eased past him, the delicate warmth of her shoulder brushing his in the process. Her lips compressing, she shook her head at him. "The babies, silly! Kids grow so fast. And clothes are expensive. So all of my siblings who have kids have been trading stuff back and forth, as is appropriate. And then when the cousins outgrow things, we put them back in storage at Mom and Dad's, and then it's there if anybody needs anything."

Made sense, Cooper thought, watching as Jillian took the lid off the first box. Pulled out a frilly pink-and-white baby dress. Another in pale blue. And then a third in sunshine yellow. She lit up just looking at the outfits. "These are so adorable! I can't wait to try them on the girls tomorrow!"

If Hallie, Sadie and Tess had been their kids, this would have been both expected and great. But Jillian was no relation to them. Not permanent, anyway. Was Cade right? Cooper wondered uncomfortably, beginning to feel like he was taking advantage of Jillian again. Even if inadvertently.

Was she starting to feel like a parent to his nieces? She was certainly looking and acting like one at the moment.

"I don't know that the girls should use these things," he said, guilt flooding through him for involving her in his sister's situation.

Jillian put the clothes down abruptly. She stared at him, two spots of color blooming across her high cheeks. Hurt gleamed in her pretty eyes. "Why not?"

"Well." He cleared his throat. Tracking the loose strands of hair escaping from her clip and grazing the elegant nape of her neck. "Like you said—" he moved close enough to drink in her rose-scented perfume "—these are Lockhart family clothes..."

She tugged him over to sit on one of the stools at the kitchen island. Dropping down beside him, she swiveled so they were facing each other. Their knees were barely grazing, but his blood still heated from having her so close, and he had to forcibly tamp down the urge to touch her when he glimpsed the hem of her skirt riding up her thighs.

"And your girls need them right now," she drawled, indignant.

"I'm not disputing that."

"Then what are you disputing exactly?" she countered, indignant.

Still holding her eyes, he shrugged. "Whose responsibility it is to take care of any shortfalls, I guess."

Her chin lifted. "Yours? Not mine."

Or *ours*, he thought, even though it felt like it should be primarily his, since he was the girls' uncle. Jillian was just a family friend.

Her soft lips compressed. She sighed and shook her head at him, then slid off the stool and marched over to pull out the rest of the items for his perusal. "I don't know if you've noticed, Coop," she began in feminine exasperation, "but they don't have much in the way of a wardrobe."

Actually, he had.

At least compared to what he and Desiree'd had as kids.

"Which is why," Jillian explained, giving him yet another long, informative look that set his pulse to racing, "I'm constantly doing baby laundry." She held up a hand before he could interrupt. "And what they do have is starting to get a little snug. So…" she said with a sniff, "this is the *perfect* solution, and like I said, none of this stuff is being used right now. But if you prefer…" She hesitated, suddenly looking as if she were close to bursting into tears. "I…" She swallowed hard, her feelings clearly hurt, and rightly so, he figured. Since he was rudely and unexpectedly finding fault with what she had tried to do for him and his nieces.

"I mean *you*, or I…could go to the baby boutique in town and purchase new garments for them." Her voice dropped an apologetic notch. "If you're uncomfortable with the idea of them wearing gently used clothing."

It was his turn to be uneasy. "Of course not," he said, embarrassed she would think his reluctance had anything to do with something as snobby as that. He held out his hands in an attempt to placate her. "I simply don't want to *take advantage*—"

Something came and went in her expression. She went very quiet and still. "You're not."

The silence between them lengthened.

She continued looking at him like she didn't know what to do or say next.

Cooper sighed. Maybe he was making a mountain out of a molehill. And maybe it was premature to be purchasing much of anything for the kids, until he saw what his sister's plans were. For one thing, the weather—and type of garb required—would be quite different one thousand miles north. "I'm sorry. I didn't mean to look a gift horse in the mouth."

Now tears *were* sparkling in her pretty blue eyes. She shook her head in barely leashed aggravation. "You're calling me a gift horse?"

A gift maybe. A rare and beautiful gift. But wary of coming across in a way that might sound insincere, he merely smiled back at her and tried again. "It was a figure of speech." One that ranchers used all the time. "Obviously, the wrong one. I didn't mean to be rude."

She sized him up, clearly aware there was more on his mind than he was allowing. Sighing, she stepped closer and asked, "But…?"

Words weren't working. So he wrapped his arms around her and pulled her toward him. Then, cupping her chin in his palm, he looked at her affectionately. "There are times when I can't help but think we all must be one giant imposition for you."

Just like that, the fight left her slender frame. She splayed her hands across his chest. Caressing even as she held him at bay. "Well, don't," she muttered.

Looking as if she couldn't decide whether to throttle him or press her lips to his. "I love having you here!" She stood on her tiptoes and kissed him. Lightly and provocatively. Winding her arms about his neck, she continued in a low, heart-rending tone, "I mean it, Coop. You and the girls have filled up my life in a way I couldn't have ever imagined."

Which was, Cooper thought morosely, *exactly* the problem.

Jillian wasn't sure what had happened to change Cooper's mood. He had been fine when they had left for the evening with her family. And seemed okay once they'd gotten to the Circle L, if a little aloof, which was understandable. Her seven siblings, their spouses and kids, plus her parents all at once would be overwhelming for anyone.

Additionally, she knew Cooper was embarrassed about the situation with his baby sister. The fact that he still didn't know what was going on in Nashville...

Nor did she, Jillian thought. But it wasn't for a lack of trying. She had been texting little updates and photos of the girls every day since they had been with her. Desiree hadn't responded in writing, but she was looking at the texts. The Read Receipts function on her cell phone confirmed that.

And that was something.

Although she hadn't mentioned what she was doing to Cooper, who was also texting his sister every day, often multiple times, to try to get her to respond. And/or set up a time when he and Desiree and possibly the girls, too, could talk for at least a few minutes.

To no avail.

Desiree had gone radio silent as far as her big brother was concerned.

So maybe that was what was bothering him, she decided, as Cooper and King slipped out the door for a little late-night fetch/walk around her property. All she knew for sure was that Cooper looked like he wanted and needed to be alone for a while. She respected that.

"We might be a while," he warned on the other side of the portal. His glance roved her tenderly. "So…if you want to go on to bed, we'll be quiet when we come in. And, of course, if the kids wake up before we get back…" He held up his phone.

She shook off his need to be on call. "I don't think they will. They were all exhausted."

"But if you *do* need me," he continued to insist, as if he were the biggest burden ever! "Just call or text, and I'll head right back to the house."

"Okay," Jillian said. Trying not to read anything more into it than there probably was.

She waited for them to leave.

Instead, he paused, brow furrowing. "I've got an early morning."

So what was he telling her? Jillian wondered, feeling even more confused. That he didn't want to make love with her, the way they usually did when they found themselves with a quiet moment alone late in the evening? Not that they had ever actually slept together for an entire night. Given their friends with benefits arrangement, they always gravitated to their own spaces at bedtime.

Though tonight she would have liked to sleep, wrapped in his arms, even if they didn't have sex.

Belatedly aware he was waiting for her reaction, she forced a smile and said, "I've got a really long day ahead of me tomorrow, too."

He nodded, retreating into small talk. "What time are the volunteers getting here in the morning?"

"Seven a.m." Not sure how much more of this awkward conversation she could take, Jillian made a show of consulting her watch. "I've got to deliver some rosebushes to a landscape center in San Angelo, so I will probably leave shortly after they arrive."

"Okay. Well, I'll be close by at my ranch should anything arise."

"I'll be sure to let them know," Jillian promised.

He and King left on their walk.

Feeling oddly near tears, Jillian went back into the house. She finished sorting through the baby clothes, then exhausted, headed upstairs. She got ready for bed and then slipped beneath the covers and turned off the lamp.

And it was only then, when she should have been sound asleep, that she heard Cooper come back inside.

The next day passed in a whirlwind of activity. Determined to get all the deliveries she had been postponing done, Jillian worked through lunch, instead choosing to have a protein bar and electrolyte drink while she drove. Her plan to condense everything into as little time away from the triplets as possible worked. With a good two hours to spare, she was headed back to Rosehaven when she approached the entrance to Cooper's Rock Creek Ranch.

And saw her mother's SUV pulling out onto the country road. Heading toward town.

Concerned something might have happened with the triplets, her gut churned. But no one had tried to contact her so she was probably jumping to the worst-case scenario, right? Then another disturbing notion occurred to her. What if her mom had taken it upon herself to have the kind of talk with Cooper she'd had with Jillian the previous day, about the false intimacy that could be generated by a family crisis…?

Turning beneath the wrought-iron archway that delineated the ranch entrance, she tried to get her racing thoughts under control as she drove toward the ranch house.

Cooper's truck was parked in front.

King was lounging on the front porch, his paws hanging over the edge.

She pulled to a stop behind Cooper's pickup and got out. King stood, tail wagging, and let out a single happy woof. Acutely aware of how grimy and sweaty she was after a day working mostly outside in the Texas heat, Jillian rubbed his silky head. "Hey there, fella," she said softly.

The front door opened. Cooper stepped out.

Like her, he looked as if he had spent the entire day outside, laboring hard.

His handsome brow furrowed. "Everything okay?"

"That's what I was going to ask you." Jillian paused, her heartrate accelerating. "Was that my mom's SUV I just saw leaving?"

He nodded, his expression unreadable.

"What's going on?" Jillian prodded with a disgruntled frown. "Why did she come by?"

He neared her, his big body filling up the space. "Why don't you come inside. Sit down and have something cold to drink."

She followed him, King trotting beside her.

Suddenly, he was all Texas gentleman. Determined to please. "Water? Soda? Tea?"

Why did she have the feeling he was stalling, buying time to figure out how to phrase whatever it was he needed to say. Ignoring the nerves tingling inside her, she dipped her head deferentially. "Iced tea. Please."

Cooper settled into his role as solicitous host. "Lemon? Sugar?"

Okay, he was *definitely* stalling. She had the pre-breakup jitters. And now her knees felt wobbly, too. "Plain is fine. Thanks."

The air conditioner was blowing full blast, so it was cool inside compared to the sizzling outdoor heat. He sat down in his lounge chair and she took the sofa that until recently had been in his sister's Dallas apartment. Glass in hand, she waited.

Maddeningly, nothing was forthcoming. It seemed if she were going to get any information out of Cooper, she was going to have to pry it from him. She turned to him, saw that his sable eyes were as worried as she felt, that a mixture of tension and regret etched the handsome planes of his face. Fury erupted inside her. "Please tell me my mother didn't quiz you about your intentions!"

His brow lifted and he gave her a quizzical look.

"About me," she said, clarifying her statement. She recalled the talk she'd had with her mother, and her mom's worry that she and Cooper might be enjoying a closeness that would fade once their reason for being together ended. As it likely would when Desiree came back to collect her children.

"No." Now it was Cooper's turn to be full-out concerned about their situation. "Does your mom know we've been…?"

Mortified at the thought, Jillian splayed a hand across her heart. "Hooking up? *Lord, no!* But she is worried about the close quarters we've been…um…

enjoying, I guess." She wasn't sure what the right word was for their cohabiting.

Cooper exhaled and kicked back on the end of the sofa. "Well, that makes two of us," he admitted thickly. "Because if we weren't under the same roof, sharing care of my nieces…"

Jillian reluctantly saw where this was going. "Then we wouldn't be hooking up?"

He gestured aimlessly, admitting, "I'm not sure we would have even been speaking, given how you used to feel about me. And what happened in the past."

Yes, they had made mistakes. Who hadn't? It was time…actually, past time…for them to move on. Not keep rehashing ancient history! "I'm over that, Cooper. Truly. I was wrong to ever blame you for any of it. You were only trying to protect me and keep me from getting hurt. I understand that now. Hell," she said, then stood and began to pace. Over to the boxed-up piles of his sister's belongings, the still unassembled cribs for the triplets, and other baby items she currently did not need or did not have room for.

Restlessly, she turned on her heel and went back to face him. "I probably understood it back then. I was just too stubborn to hear it."

He grinned at her self-effacing explanation. "You were a little obstinate," he teased.

She knew he wanted to change the subject. But she wasn't about to let him off the hook that easily.

She knotted her hands in front of her. "It still doesn't explain why my mother was here."

His forehead furrowed. He stood and went over to retrieve more iced tea. "I called her and asked her to come by," he reported in a low, thoroughly reasonable tone. "I wanted to talk to her privately and unofficially about my family situation. See what my options were going to be if Desiree doesn't come back after all."

So he'd been calling on her mother for her social worker expertise. Jillian jerked in a calming breath. "And?"

He gave her a telling look. Then coolly topped off his glass. "She agreed I can't bring the triplets into a construction zone. It's just way too dangerous right now."

The heat within her cooled. She was still on edge, but considerably less so. Trying to help solve the problem with him, she asked, "Would the situation change if you were able to get the downstairs finished and gate off the stairs to the second floor?"

His gaze caressed her face. "Yes, but to get it done swiftly would require me getting a construction loan/second mortgage and hiring contractors. And that would all take time I don't really have. Plus Hallie, Sadie, Tess and I would still need some place to live—like an apartment in town—which would make work on the ranch all the more difficult..."

She waved off his concern. "You-all could continue to stay with me."

The grooves on either side of his lips deepened. "I appreciate your generosity, Jillian." He drained his glass and set it aside, then turned back to her, every bit as resolute as she was. "But at some point," he continued gravely, "you are going to resent the way your life has been turned upside down by all this."

She tensed, trying not to cry. "What makes you think that?"

"Because," Cooper said gruffly, "I've been in this situation before. When I was named Desiree's legal guardian. And I accepted way too much help from my very kind and generous high school sweetheart."

Jillian blinked. Then asked incredulously, "You moved in with her?"

Cooper shook his head. "Linda moved in with *us*," he corrected. "And she and I got married."

Chapter Twelve

Jillian stared at Cooper in shock. How on earth had this not come out before? And why did it hurt so much hearing about it? She set her glass down with a thud, for a moment feeling like she was facing off with a total stranger. "You were *married*?" she echoed incredulously. "At eighteen?"

"Yep." He moved away from her and began to pace. "For about a year."

Not sure her knees would support her at that moment, Jillian remained where she was, her hands folded tightly in her lap. She studied the taut lines of his handsome profile. "I'm guessing it didn't go well."

He rubbed the back of his neck and swung back to face her. The day's beard gave him a ruggedly masculine look. "That was the thing." His dark eyes shimmered. "It went incredibly well at first."

He lifted his shoulders in an indolent shrug. "I guess it was the honeymoon period. Because we both went overboard trying to make each other happy, and be there for Desiree, too." He exhaled heavily. "The problem was, Desiree didn't want a mother replacement, or a big sister."

Jillian sympathized. "How did Linda take that?" she asked quietly.

Cooper scrubbed a hand over his face. As the silence drew out, he shook his head, reflecting, "At first, she was really patient and understanding, more so than I was able to be, given how difficult Desiree was being about literally everything. But eventually my sister's never-ending attitude and outright defiance got under Linda's skin. The two quarreled constantly." He grimaced. "Initially, I was asked to be referee and decide who was right and who was wrong."

Compassion welled within her. Steadily, she held Cooper's gaze. "That hardly seems fair."

"It wasn't," he admitted curtly. His gaze drifted over her, generating little sparks of desire wherever it landed. "Because no matter who I sided with, I lost." Frustration edged his low tone. "And it seemed as if I was expected to support *someone* on every issue. Bottom line? What started out as a 'fairy tale' marriage eventually became as toxic as my little sister's relationship with everyone around her. And eventually Linda—who had given up college to run off with me—decided to cut her losses and go back to building a future for herself on her own. So, we divorced, and that was that."

Jillian shook her head at all he had been through. "You must have been heartbroken," she whispered.

Jaw taut, Cooper edged nearer. "I think I was more relieved." His lips compressed ruefully. "By then, I knew I had proposed out of a mixture of grief and a need to somehow make things better for my baby sister." He folded his arms, his biceps bulging beneath the rumpled fabric of his tan work shirt. "Linda and I were great as teenage boyfriend and girlfriend, but in the long run, we were never going to make each other happy. The best thing to do was cut ties. Move on with our lives."

Wishing they had the kind of relationship that would allow her to simply hold him close in a situation like this, Jillian reached for her drink and sipped the cool liquid, hoping to ease the sudden dryness in her throat. Briefly, her glance shifted to the impressive muscles in his chest and shoulders, before returning to his face. Gently, she asked, "Did things get better with Desiree after that?"

"No." His expression darkening, he admitted, "And that was at least partially my fault, too. I was trying too hard to be both father and mother and big brother to her. She resented being told what to do. So we fought all the more. This time without Linda as buffer."

Their eyes met and held. "I'm sorry about all that."

Glad you're finally telling me the whole story, instead of just selected bits and pieces, here and there. But...

She rose gracefully. Still not understanding. And released a tremulous breath as she stepped closer to him. "What does everything that happened then have to do with you and me now?"

Everything. Nothing, Cooper thought, inhaling the faintly antiseptic scent of the hand soap she used after working in the greenhouse, combined with the salty tang of perspiration and the neutral fragrance of her sunscreen. All mingled with the unique aroma of Jillian's hair and skin and made him want nothing more than to ravish her, right then and there.

"You and I entered into an intimate relationship for all the wrong reasons, too." Which was why they shouldn't give in to the desire that simmered between them whenever they were close. Even now...

Jillian propped her hands on her hips. She dug in stubbornly, glaring at him all the while. "I thought we had established that we are both adults who understand the ramifications of our actions. And can do as we please." Her lower lip took on that feisty curve he recalled so well.

"Don't you think I wish that all I had to do was kiss you again, and then miraculously all our problems would just melt away?" he countered, frustrated to find her making it even harder on them by refusing to see reason.

She shrugged and batted her eyelashes at him. "Even if they don't magically go away, I'd still like a kiss."

Her attempt to ease him out of his worries failed.

He knew how she hated to overthink things. But in this case, it was necessary to examine what was really going on here. And think about the negative impact it could have to all their futures.

Cooper called on every ounce of gallantry he possessed. He could see that Jillian was still up for some lovemaking, but after the way he had inadvertently hurt Linda, did he really want to hurt Jillian, too?

And she was in a position to really be hurt. He knew that now.

"We're also playing at being a family. Temporarily," he added gruffly.

Seeing she was about to argue the point, he released a harsh breath and said, "At least that's what it felt like last night when we were at your folks' ranch."

Indignation flickered in her expression. Followed swiftly by a resentment that seemed to go soul-deep. "And that bothers you?" she countered crisply.

Hell, yes, it bothered him! He regarded her steadily. "I know you were hurt before in a convenient relationship with the guy you dated in college."

"So?"

"I don't want to similarly use you. And if this

is…" He paused, searching for a way to describe it. "False closeness—or situational intimacy—the kind people experience when they go through some sort of traumatic event together, then I—"

Appearing abruptly relieved, she cut him off with a light touch of her hand. Everything about her demeanor gentling, she stepped closer, promising sweetly, "If that's the case, Coop—and for the record, I don't think it is—but if it *is*, then you're right. We'll realize it eventually. And deal with whatever our circumstances are at the time. As adults."

She sounded so matter-of-fact about the possibility that their reckless romantic entanglement might blow up in their faces. And while his conscience would have liked to simply accept her reassurance, that she could indeed handle such a disappointment, everything he knew about her to date still made him wary.

"The choices being…if we do—" again he had to search for the most inoffensive words "—decide to stop hooking up…?"

She slanted him a sultry look from beneath her lashes. Shifted even closer. "Well, maybe we'll stay friends. Which is what I hope."

Unable to help himself, he reached out to tuck an errand strand of honey-blond hair behind her ear. "Me, too," Cooper admitted gruffly.

She turned her face into his palm, luxuriating in the skin-to-skin contact. Then mischievously looked into his eyes, murmuring seductively, "Possibly even lovers…"

Liking the direction of her thoughts, he fought to contain the hardness pressing against his fly, and flashed her a wicked smile. "Can't say I'd mind that…" he rasped.

Jillian rested her hands on his shoulders and went on as seductively as he had come to expect. "The point is, Coop, we don't have a crystal ball. We don't know what the future holds. All we can do is take it one step, one *day*, at a time. Do our best by the girls to give them as much stability and security as we can right now. And have faith that in time everything will work out for the best." She hugged him, their embrace fueled with pent-up desire. Then stepped back.

He felt her physical absence acutely.

Which made him realize she wasn't the only one who was likely to be hurt if their relationship ended, along with their temporary custody of the babies.

Gazing at her, he stated a little more brusquely than he intended, "It's a little hard to believe everything is going to magically work out when we don't know what Desiree is going to do next."

His bitterness conjured up Jillian's usual empathy—for the other side. Patiently, she reminded him, "Desiree probably doesn't know, either. Yet."

Cooper wished he were one-tenth as understanding. But right now, all he could think of was the potential damage being done to the kids. The possibility that Sadie, Tess and Hallie might very well be in the process of being abandoned by the only parent they had—even if he and Jillian were loathe to admit that just yet. He shook his head grimly. "That doesn't make Desiree's lack of communication with us okay."

Jillian took his hand and held it between them. She clasped his fingers tightly, reassuringly, in hers. "I know it's frustrating, Coop. I'm feeling that way, too."

As he looked at her face, he could see that was true.

She drew a deep breath that lifted the soft swell of her breasts. Even more resolutely, she forged on. "Because—like you, cowboy—I'm used to just stepping in and taking charge of a situation." She shook her head sadly. "And we can't do that here. Not yet." They exchanged glances and she offered a fragile smile. "What we *can* do is take it one step at a time. The way your dad always advised. Be patient and understanding and hope for the best." She tightened her grip on his hand.

He seized the moment to lever her intimately close. She had such a huge heart. Bigger than his, that was for certain. "You are incredible, you know that?" Wrapping one arm about her waist, he bent down and kissed her temple tenderly. She felt so good against him. So warm and giving.

Like she wanted nothing more than to surrender to whatever this was between them. *Again.*

They had another hour before they had to be back at Rosehaven...

She beamed under his praise. "If I weren't so hot and sweaty and smelly—" she raised herself to kiss his lips "—I'd haul you off to bed."

Bed sounded mighty fine. He tucked an arm beneath her knees and swung her up into his arms. Holding her against his chest, he headed for the stairs. "Well, you're in luck then, darlin'." He paused to kiss her again, deeply and passionately this time. Not stopping until she was kissing him back with equal fervor. Finally, lifting his head, he winked. "I've got a shower. Just big enough for two."

It seemed to take forever for them to get all the way up the stairs, because Cooper kept stopping to kiss her. And every time his lips claimed hers, she couldn't help but kiss him back as thoroughly and hungrily as he was kissing her.

Finally, they were in his bathroom.

Clothes were coming off.

He wrapped his hands around her waist, all hot possessive male. She saw the kiss coming as he backed her into the shower just big enough for two. And it was everything she expected it would be. Tender and giving, seductive and hot, unbearably sensual. Demanding.

Pure happiness flowing through her, she wound her arms about his neck, pressed her breasts against his chest and lower still, arched into him wantonly.

Luxuriating in the salty male scent of him, she purred, "Got any soap?"

He grinned, his eagerness to possess her apparent as the slick moisture between her thighs. "You want to play?"

"Oh, yeah." She took the bar of the soap he handed her and lathered it between her fingers. "You bring out the impish side of me." Using the tips of her fingers, she spread the lather across his shoulders and chest, down the goody trail to his navel and below. He groaned as she spread soap across his hips, between his thighs. And especially, *there*.

With a groan of raw, guttural delight, he took the soap from her palm. Pressing her back against the wall. "My turn."

Determined, it seemed, to have all of her, he lathered her body head to toe, front to back, lingering over her swelling breasts and nipples, the small of her back, the nest of curls and the inside of her thighs.

As he noticed the depth of her enjoyment, his own pleasure grew. Cupping the hard, velvety hot length of him in her palm, she reached for the detachable shower nozzle with her free hand. "Time for a rinse…"

He growled with arousal as she lovingly dispensed with all the bubbles. Front to back.

"My turn…" He did the same for her. Wet, clean, they came together again, both fully under the nozzle this time. Her nipples beaded. The damp throbbing between her legs intensified as she concentrated on all that was good and right between them.

Cooper's body ached with the need to possess Jillian.

He slipped from the shower just long enough to retrieve a condom, then returned, taking her in his arms and kissing her in the all-consuming way they both loved. Determined to make her see what they could have if she only lowered her guard and let him all the way into her heart, he deepened their kiss even more. Her body trembled as he filled her. Surrendering to him with the sweet passion of a woman who was destined to be his, she clasped him to her. Opening more. Allowing him to lift her and press her against the shower wall. Trapping her against his seductive heat. Their bodies merged. Then rocking seductively against him, she stared into his eyes, encouraging him to go deep, deeper still. Taking as she gave and giving him more in return. The tender yearning pouring out of him and her. Until she peaked, exquisitely and erotically, and he laid claim to her lips and body as he wanted to lay claim to her heart and soul.

Jillian and Cooper came back to earth slowly as the aftershocks faded. The only sound in the bathroom, the uneven exhales of their breaths and the mesmerizing sound of the warm water still sluicing over them.

Cooper stroked her hair, kissed her temple, the curve of her cheek.

Her head on his shoulder, Jillian worked to steady herself. Bring strength back into her still-wobbly knees.

She wished they could stay like this forever, snuggling wordlessly. Because when they were together like this, it felt so right, so *real*, and all her doubts slid away.

It was only when their real life crowded in—their work obligations, their families, the uncertainty of the future—that she began to feel uneasy. And worry she was once again opening her heart up too easily, too soon.

Because despite what she'd told Cooper about this being a temporary friends-with-benefits situation, she couldn't help but want more from this. From him. And he seemed to be wanting and needing more from her, too.

The question was, would they be able to give it?

He had said he wasn't interested in getting married or having kids, at the outset.

That he liked being a single rancher with a dog.

And if the woman he was seeing didn't understand that, then, well…the relationship ended, and he moved on, apparently no worse for the breakup.

That alone was enough to force her to continue to still be cautious.

But there was more.

She had her own issues, too.

Since her parents had perished in the fire and she had been put in foster care, she'd resisted loving anyone else. That had changed a little when she had been adopted by Robert and Carol. And reunited with her siblings.

But she knew deep down she was still afraid that if she let herself fully embrace the new life she was finding with Cooper and the girls, that disaster would strike once again. She'd lose everything. And everyone. And suffer the worst broken heart imaginable in the process.

Chapter Thirteen

Two and a half weeks later...

"I don't know. What do you think?" Jillian asked Cooper, enjoying their time together, as the five of them gathered around the round dining table in the Wagon Wheel restaurant. "Do you think it would be okay to give the girls french fries?"

Looking as content as she felt, he grinned at the way Sadie kept reaching for his.

Tess was doing the same thing to Jillian's plate. Even the picky Hallie looked intrigued.

"Maybe if we cut them into tiny pieces?" he suggested finally.

They worked to divvy up a crispy potato wedge

for each girl. Put them in front of them. Then watched as the exploration began.

Sadie got a bite in her mouth, spit it out, looked at it, then put it right back in again.

Hallie put it to her lips, then pushed it away.

Tess nibbled delicately on a morsel. Dropped it. Picked up another and did the same.

Watching, a burst of maternal contentment soared through her. Maybe she was more of a natural mom than she knew. "Well, that's pretty good for the first time, don't you think?" Jillian said. Once again, she was aware what a good team she and Cooper made.

Cooper grinned affectionately at the girls, then turned that same affection back to her. "I do. And," he drawled, picking up his burger, "there is the added bonus of keeping them busy while we eat..."

She shifted in her chair. Beneath the table, their knees touched. "Good point, cowboy," she teased amiably. "Although we have gotten pretty good at multitasking and working everything in," Jillian bragged, cutting into her grilled chicken.

Cooper chuckled and gave her a leisurely once-over. "Life is definitely better and getting more so every day," he reflected happily, sipping his iced tea.

Jillian felt herself flush at his thoroughly male attention.

Thanks to the help of the volunteer babysitters from the Multiples Club, both of them had been able to get their businesses back on track. The triplets were thriving, too. And to her delight, she and Cooper were getting closer than ever. In part, due to all the time they spent mutually caring for the girls, every morning and evening. And then, there were the quiet moments, talking about nothing and everything, coupled with the fact they made hot, passionate love nearly every night...

"Want to go to the park after this?" Cooper asked, as he paid the bill for their meals.

More "family" time. Jillian smiled. "I'd love it, and so would the girls."

He carried Hallie and Tess. She toted Sadie.

As luck would have it, the bucket swings for babies were full, so they let the girls play in the big sandbox instead, using the community pails and shovels and trucks that were a permanent fixture of the playground.

Jillian and Cooper sat shoulder to shoulder on one of the parent benches that rimmed the area, watching over them.

She snapped a photo of the girls playing and texted it to him, knowing she would send it to Desiree later, too.

Not that the triplets' mother had ever replied to one of the photos.

But Jillian knew Desiree was still opening every text from the Read Receipts.

And that was something.

It meant Desiree had not abandoned her children entirely, the way Cooper seemed to fear...

In the distance, the sky took on a streaky pink

at the horizon. A comfortably warm breeze wafted over them. It was such a pretty evening. So peaceful and tranquil…

"You know, I've been thinking," Cooper said eventually, smiling when Sadie filled her bucket with sand, dumped it out and started all over again.

He draped an arm along the back of the bench, drawing her into the warm, solid curve of his body. Then leaned over to murmur in her ear, "As much as I enjoy coming into town in the evenings for dinner and playground time—" which had become their habit since both had gone back to work full-time "—I think it would be nice if we had baby swings for them at the ranch, too."

Jillian turned toward him, her shoulder and the curve of her breast pressing up against his side. A tingle of awareness swept through her, mingling with the ease their togetherness always engendered. "Are you thinking about hanging them from a tree branch?" She had several big sturdy live oaks in her yard.

Cooper cocked his head. "Actually, there is a 'gently used' metal swing set for sale on the Laramie Multiples Club exchange board." He held up a hand before she could get too excited. "It's pretty simple. No slide or glider. But it would accommodate three bucket swings, side by side, which is all we would need. And the frame can be installed with anchors that you pound into the ground. So, if you wanted to move it to another location, or exchange

it for something more complex or high end, it could
be done easily."

She studied the reserve in his brown eyes, yet his
trepidation was pointless because she truly wanted
to help out in any way she could. "Are you trying to
ask me if I want to put it at Rosehaven?"

His shoulders relaxed with relief. "That would be
the most convenient location for now." He looked
at her lovingly before continuing. "And like I said,
the whole thing could later be quickly and easily removed. So you wouldn't have to worry about a lot of
damage to your yard or anything like that."

He was so overly considerate of her, it was almost comical. She aimed a thumb at the center of
her chest. "That's me, all right, cowboy. I lay awake
nights worrying about how the grass looks."

He tipped back his head and laughed, the velvety rough sound filling the evening air. Shaking
his head ruefully, he turned back to her. "I think
you know what I mean, darlin'. You're a botanist,
and a damn fine one at that. You take these things
very seriously. And you have a very nice, very well-
manicured yard."

She nudged his knee with her own, acknowledging drolly, "As a person who makes her living via
her plant expertise, I kind of have to. But...thank
you." It felt good to know he respected her as much
as she respected him.

His eyes crinkled at the corners. "You're welcome."

"Mmm! Dddd! 'Ook!" Hallie suddenly shouted.

They both grinned as Hallie abandoned her shovel altogether and put handfuls of sand into her bucket.

"Ma! Da! Me!" Sadie ran circles around the interior of the sandbox.

Not to be outdone, Tess—who rarely spoke anything but the triplets baby babble that only the three of them could understand—suddenly stood and proclaimed loudly, "Mom! Dad!"

Caught off guard by the clarity of what they had all just said, Jillian gasped. Her eyes filled with happy tears that were followed swiftly by equal amounts of guilt and confusion.

Looking equally touched and worried, Cooper turned to her. "Do you think they're really starting to view us as their official parents?" he asked hoarsely.

If that were the case, Jillian wasn't surprised. The two of them had certainly temporarily done their best to assume the roles of loving guardians to the girls. "I don't know," she said honestly as Hallie climbed out of the sandbox and came over to give Jillian a handful of sand.

"Thank you," she said.

"Mmmm!" Hallie turned and went back to play with her sisters.

"So was that…an early version of 'Momma'?" Cooper asked.

"I'm not sure. I mean, I know when they play with the 'cousins' at my parents' ranch on the weekend, they hear all the other kids saying 'Mommy' and 'Daddy' constantly, but to assume…at sixteen months…they know what a mother or father is might be stretching it."

Cooper nodded, accepting that.

Figuring to continue the discussion would be to step into an emotional minefield, Jillian cleared her throat.

They had avoided talking about Desiree. It was such a sore subject with him. A fact that made her continued secret texts to his sister a little on the risky side. Because if that blew up for any reason… He would likely be angry with her. Of that she was sure.

"Back to your wish to put in a swing set at Rose-haven. Did anything prompt this decision?" Jillian asked.

His expression hardened. "It's been four weeks now and except for the texted pediatrician info, when the triplets were ill, I have yet to hear a peep from my sister."

Jillian's breath hitched in her chest. "She warned it could be two to four weeks in the letter she left you." She reached over and took Cooper's hand.

"I understand that she may not know yet exactly what she wants to do. But for my own sake…for my need to be in control rather than at the mercy of someone else's whims…"

Whims? Jillian thought.

That made it sound more frivolous than it was.

Cooper swallowed. He turned a pensive glance to the horizon. "I need to start thinking about what will happen if Desiree doesn't come back for another few months or even longer."

He shook his head. Tightening his fingers in hers. "I need to be able to take care of the girls on my own. If it comes to that, and… I want the situation right now to be more permanent."

This was the first glimmer he might want to take on actual legal custody of his nieces. Hope filled Jillian's heart. "Do you want that?" she asked softly, swiveling to face him.

He made a seesawing motion, his expression conflicted. "I think I need to be prepared for whatever happens. So the options will be there."

Jillian knew that Cooper was still privately hopeful that his sister would return and be the kind of mother the triplets needed. So the two of them could give up the temporary mom and dad roles. She just wasn't sure how realistic that was. And she also wanted what was best for the girls. "I agree. Tess, Sadie and Hallie need to be protected. An emergency plan made." She swallowed around the sudden lump in her throat. "So they don't end up like my siblings and I did. At the mercy of the foster care system."

"That's why I have been talking to the bank. I'm going to go ahead and get a construction loan mortgage on the Rock Creek, and finish the remodel now, rather than waiting to do it one step at a time."

Jillian's eyes widened in shock. This was big. Even if she wasn't sure what it meant for her when it came to him and the girls. Was he looking for an eventual way out of their arrangement? A return to his bachelor existence? She felt pressure building behind her eyes. "I think that's wise. And a little surprising," she couldn't help but add.

His expression inscrutable, he conceded, "I'll admit, at first taking care of three baby girls was more than overwhelming. It seemed impossible. But thanks to your help, and the volunteers pitching in, and the advice of your mom…"

Jillian blinked, interrupting curiously, *"My mom?"*

Cooper flicked a glance her way. "The day I asked Carol to come over, she told me that the worst thing I could do in a situation like this was rush into, or out of, anything. That some of the time, things would get sorted out all on their own. And there were other times when they wouldn't." He released a breath. "But in the meantime, the Department of Children and Family Services in Laramie had all sort of ways to assist families in need of external support. Everything from lists of places where I could get discounted child care, family counseling and legal advice, to single parent support groups. She said even if all I needed was a listening ear, her door was always open. And that if we had a need, she would figure out a way to fill it."

"Wow," Jillian mused. She was a little embarrassed she'd thought her mom had only been there to interfere in her love life. She really hadn't given her enough credit.

"At the time I was sure this was going to be a

temporary situation, so I took her offer with a grain of salt, but now…" Cooper said with a sigh, entwining his fingers with hers, "I'm thinking they might be with me a lot longer. Maybe even permanently if the situation doesn't change."

Jillian gazed down at their clasped hands. His hand was much larger than hers; yet the two fit perfectly. Was this a sign of better things to come? Or just wishful thinking on her part?

She inhaled deeply, forcing herself to keep her guard up just a little and not to rush into anything. "Hopefully, Desiree will come back and the two of you can iron out your differences. And figure out a way for all of you to be family from here on out." Because that really would be best.

He flashed a crooked smile. Lifted her hand to his lips and kissed the back of it. "Yeah, well, here's hoping," he interjected gruffly. "In the meantime," he said, "what would you think about the two of us arranging for a babysitter and going on a real date?"

Jillian's heart swelled in her chest. "I'd love it."

Neither one of them wanted to wait, once the decision was made, so they settled on the next evening. Jillian's "wild child" baby sister, Emma, finally back permanently from her footwear apprenticeship in Italy, was going to babysit.

"Triplets already in bed?" Emma asked, setting down her carryall with a sketchpad peeking out of the top.

Grateful for her youngest sister's help, Jillian nodded. "I gave them an abbreviated afternoon nap so I could feed them and put them down early. They've been asleep since seven."

Emma ran a hand through the silky blond mane that hung nearly to her waist. "What time is Cooper going to be here?"

He had been at his ranch all day and planned to shower and get ready there, then come to Rosehaven. Hoping he would be as game as always when he found out what she now had on their agenda, she said, "Anytime."

Emma frowned. "Shouldn't you change, then?" Her gaze swept Jillian's work clothes.

"Actually, there's been a change of plans," she confided proudly. "I got a call from the governor's mansion. Texas's First Lady wants one hundred of my hardiest Old Blush rosebushes, but only if they can be delivered by noon tomorrow."

Emma, who was usually all about work, remained unimpressed. "So? Go on the date and work all night, if you have to!"

It wasn't that simple, unfortunately. Jillian headed for her kitchen. "I'm going to need his help. Or someone's." Though she really didn't want to call someone else…she wanted to spend time alone with Cooper. Even if they were working!

Emma stared at her, disappointed. "You're really going to forego your very first, very special actual first date with him…for time in your greenhouse?"

Aware her little sister was all about fashion, not agriculture, Jillian said, "Cooper will understand." At least she hoped so, she thought fervently, making a picnic dinner of sandwiches, chips, apples and a big jug of iced tea.

Emma slid onto a stool. She picked a fresh peach from the bowl on the counter and bit into it. "What if he doesn't? What if he's like Tom, and says it's either me or your work? What then?"

Jillian knew her sister had never gotten over her high school sweetheart, Tom Reid, breaking up with her. With a shake of her head, she reiterated, "Cooper won't do that."

Emma scoffed. "I didn't think Tom would." She recollected miserably. "But he did..."

Jillian put the picnic dinner into the wicker basket. "You're still not over him, are you?"

With a frown, Emma corrected archly, "Over the hurt he inflicted, and no, I'm not!" She stared down at her half-eaten peach. "I thought we had a forever and ever love, that we were going to see the world together, only to have him abandon me to stay right here in Laramie County."

Jillian went over and engulfed her sister in a one-armed hug. "He didn't really have a choice, Emma," she reminded her quietly. "Tom's dad died, and his mom needed help on the ranch."

Emma tilted her chin. "*That*, I understood. His refusal to even try the long-distance thing so I could still pursue *my* dreams was something else." Bitterness crept into her low tone. "Especially when he turned right around and married and had three kids with someone else."

Jillian had never thought that was a love match. More like a rebound romance that turned unexpectedly permanent, due to pregnancy. "His wife died of cancer. He's had a rough time. You need to forgive him," she said.

Emma teared up and turned away. She folded her arms in front of her. "Look, all I'm saying is that you may think Cooper is the greatest most understanding guy in the entire world right now." She paced back and forth. "But this is your first actual date. It's a *big* deal. And you're blowing it off like it was nothing!"

Was she?

Unease filled Jillian.

Cooper was a great guy, true.

But he could also totally withdraw into his strong silent shell when he was hurt or disappointed by someone close to him, the way he had been with his sister, Desiree.

Wasn't that why she had kept secret the fact she had been texting his sister photos and updates about the girls for weeks now? Because she hadn't known how he would feel about her trying to bridge the gap between him and Desiree, and was afraid to really test the waters and find out?

Jillian heard the front door open and close. The sound of a dog padding in. Then, heavy masculine footsteps moving across the wooden floor, heading their way.

Emma was still looking at her. Coming closer, she said softly, *urgently*, "It's not too late. You could still change your mind. If you pretend that you're just running a little behind…getting ready…and go upstairs and change now, he would never even be the wiser…"

Cooper lifted an inquisitive brow. "The wiser about what?" he asked, walking over to where she and her sister were huddled, King at his side.

Chapter Fourteen

Jillian had to admit it—Cooper looked incredibly handsome in a sport coat and slacks. He smelled good, too, like wintergreen and spice. Acutely aware of her own loose denim shirt, khaki shorts and sneakers, Jillian swallowed. "The fact I need to take a rain check on our date."

His dark eyes immediately filled with concern. "Everything okay with the kids?"

Her heart skittering in her chest, she drew in another whiff of his tantalizing aftershave. "Yes. I gave them an abbreviated afternoon nap so I could feed them and put them down early. They've been asleep since seven."

Hands shoved in the pockets of his slacks, he ambled closer. "Then…?" His brow furrowed.

Briefly, she told him about the request for one hundred antique rosebushes. "Apparently, the ones that arrived this morning were not up to par, so the First Lady of Texas asked around and was told my 1930's Old Blush were the very best in the state."

He shared her joy. "Congratulations."

"Thanks." She was glad he seemed to understand what a very big deal this was. She cleared her throat, ignoring the continued disapproval of her sister Emma, and went on, "The catch was, they need the antique roses by noon tomorrow. Susie Carrigan-McCabe, at the landscape center in town, agreed to have one of her guys here at six a.m. to pick the shipment up and drive it to the governor's mansion in one of her trucks. But the bushes have to be ready to go at six a.m. to ensure we meet the time frame."

Emma walked up to put in her two cents. "I told her she should go on you-all's date and then work all night."

"Which I would love to do…" Jillian said.

"But it's just not practical," Coop guessed.

Emma rolled her eyes. "You-all are killing me!" she complained.

"Says the worst workaholic of the three of us," Jillian teased back.

"Well, that's because work is all I have right now. Although—" Emma lifted her index finger in the air "—I'm *thinking* about getting a dog…"

"Always a good thing to do," Cooper agreed.

Sensing his help was needed, King padded over to stand next to Emma. Smiling, she petted him.

"So," Cooper asked Jillian, "want my help with this?"

She drew a deep breath. He really was the most chivalrous man she had ever met. She surveyed the enticing, sensual gleam in his eyes. "Would you mind?"

Cooper wrapped his arm around her shoulders, pulling her close. He gazed down at her affectionately. "Time spent with you…is always time well spent." He kissed the top of her head. "Just let me run upstairs and change."

He left. Emma fanned herself as if she were in the midst of a swoon. Then mugged at Jillian.

"Stop," Jillian hissed. Flushing, she finished packing up the dinner she'd made for them, then closed the top of the wicker basket with a snap.

"Okay, but mark my words." Her sister handed over the fancy lemon bars she had forgotten. "If you mess this up because your priorities are in the wrong place, you will regret it."

Twenty minutes later, Jillian and Cooper were in the greenhouse where the coveted plants were grown. He had changed into an old T-shirt and khaki shorts. Sneakers. Suitable for the warm, humid air inside the building. He looked relaxed, happy and sexy as hell. So much so the impetuous, romantic side of her wished she'd taken Emma's advice and gone on that pivotal first date with him...

A ghost of a smile crossed his mouth. "So what is so special about Old Blush roses?" he asked, assembling the shipping boxes.

Realizing that being alone together like this, without the buffer of kids, was nearly as intimate as an evening out would have been, Jillian drew in a deep breath. "It was in all the earliest gardens in Texas, dating back to at least 1830." She wet the soil in each container while making sure the top leaves on the plant remained dry. Doing her best to appear oblivious to his easy masculine appraisal, she bent her head over her task and continued informatively, "It's ever blooming, which means it has blossoms from early spring to late fall. It's also hardy and does well in hot, humid Texas weather."

He chuckled. "Like you?"

She had known the flirting would come. It was a good thing she was as adept at it as he was.

"And you." Jillian made a silly face at him, watching his grin widen appreciatively.

Their eyes locked for a playful moment.

It would be so easy, she thought, to get completely off-task...

He knew it, too.

But with one hundred rosebushes to pack up and only the two of them to do it...

Sobering, he cleared his throat. "I guess we better get on with this," he said.

Her awareness of him growing as much as her desire, Jillian drew in a breath. "Agreed."

Still feeling a little intoxicated by his assistance, she slipped the black plastic container into a plastic bag. Then secured it around the base of the plant, right where the roots and the top of the plant met with nursery twine. Finished, she put it in the shipping carton. Picked up another. To her delight, she and Cooper worked together, preparing the next nine or ten plants, then left the top of the box open, to provide maximum airflow to the plants, and went on to the next.

"I imagine this will really be a boost to your business," he remarked, as they slipped into a surprisingly easy and efficient rhythm.

"I hope so." Jillian drew the back of her hand across her damp forehead, blotting away the thin film of perspiration. How was it he didn't appear the least bit affected by either the heat or the exertion? "Although I don't know how I would handle any more." She sighed.

Grinning, Cooper reached over to wipe a smudge of planting soil from her cheek. "You could always hire staff to help you meet demand," he suggested as he stepped back.

She flushed, still tingling from his touch. "I don't want to try and grow too fast." That could be the death knell for a small business.

"I hear you. Most days I don't need anyone to help me manage my herd. When I do, I hire a couple of cowboys for the day or week. Whatever is needed. They're happy for the extra pay. I don't have to worry about having enough work to keep them busy or money to pay them on a regular basis."

"The joys and burdens of being self-employed and running your own business."

He nodded, still holding her gaze, and in that instant, the connection she felt seemed much deeper than mere friendship or sex or mutual concern over the kids. It felt like they were on the precipice of something much, much more complicated and long-lasting. Which again gave her pause. Were either of them ready for that? And what about the triplets? Were they ready for whatever they would face next?

Aware there were still so many unanswered questions about their future, and no way to get them just yet, she reached over to take his hand in hers. Squeezed, even as her heart somersaulted in her chest. She was so close to falling irrevocably in love with him. "I really am sorry about tonight," she told him softly, savoring the warmth and strength of his hand engulfing hers. "I'll make it up to you."

The corners of his sensual lips lifted, reminding her just how well and thoroughly he could kiss. "I am sure you will."

Emma had been right; they should have had the date first, then this. Even if it meant she was up, alone, packing roses for shipment till dawn. For no reason she could figure, her nipples were tingling.

"Where were you planning on taking me tonight, by the way?"

His brown eyes lit up. "The Laramie Country Inn."

She groaned, lamenting with dramatic flair, "Of course! The most exquisite food in the *entire* county."

"It'll still be there when we can go." Using his leverage on her fingers to tug her even closer, he leaned down to kiss her gently. Persuasively. The sizzle spread from her chest all the way to her knees.

She swayed against him, fervently returning each sipping caress.

Finally, he tore his lips from hers and drew back. The promise to pick this up again later was on his face. "In the meanwhile, let's get this done so you'll be ready to ship this precious cargo first thing tomorrow."

Eager to be alone with him, purely for fun this time, Jillian nodded. "Let's do it," she said.

It took another two hours with a short dinner break in between, but finally they were all done. Her back and shoulders aching, Jillian stepped outside the greenhouse door and stretched.

Cooper slanted her a tender look. "Stiff?" he asked.

Jillian groaned.

He stepped behind her. Massaged her shoulders and the base of her neck. "Oh, that feels good..." Jillian murmured.

He lifted the veil of her hair to one side and kissed the nape of her neck, made a lazy trail across her collarbone, up to her ear. "You know what else would feel good?"

Jillian turned to face him. She pressed her body tight against his and wound her arms around his neck. "I know lots and lots of things that would feel good," she said, lifting her lips to his once again.

Jillian's cell phone buzzed. Once and then again.

She and Cooper exchanged perplexed frowns and drew apart.

"Uh-oh." She pulled out her phone, saw Emma's name on the screen and knew it had to be something or her younger sister would not have buzzed her.

Cooper lifted a brow. "The kids?"

"I don't know." Jillian hit the green button on the screen, accepting the call. "Hey, sis. What's up?"

"Um," Emma said, sounding stressed. "Can you and Cooper get up to the house right away? We've got company."

"Expecting anyone?" Cooper asked Jillian as they threaded their way through the rows between the dozen greenhouses that comprised the Rosehaven flower operation.

Jillian's brow knit in the same confusion he was feeling. "Not this late at night."

He checked his watch. It was nearly ten thirty.

She slanted him a curious glance from beneath her lashes. Reminding him that for the last month they had been practically living together. "You?"

He shook his head. Then came to a dead stop as

they reached the expanse of lawn that separated Jillian's home from her business. A stretch limo was parked in the drive.

Desiree was sitting on the porch with Emma. The two were conversing with what looked to be a good deal of awkwardness, which wasn't surprising under the circumstances. What did you say to a woman who had deserted her three babies for the last four weeks without bothering to call and check on them?

Emma rose, looking relieved. "King and I will just go inside," she murmured, gesturing for the dog to follow. Tail wagging, King stood, and they departed while Cooper continued to stand there, like he was seeing a ghost, and not a particularly welcome one at that.

Wary of what was to come, Jillian flushed. "I should let you have some privacy, too," she said self-consciously.

Cooper caught her wrist before she could leave, his grip warm and implacable. "Stay."

"Yes," Desiree agreed, giving Jillian a woman-to-woman look that indicated she feared family fireworks as much as Jillian. "Please do," she said in a beautiful, lyrical voice.

With a reluctant nod of consent, Jillian took one of the cushioned wicker chairs on the porch. Desiree remained on the chain-hung swing. And for long moments, a tense silence ensued.

So many things were running through Cooper's mind. An equal number of emotions suffused his heart. He wanted to hug his little sister. It had been ten years after all. But she didn't seem to want that, so… Resisting the urge to chide her for having stayed away so long, he pulled up a chair instead and faced off with her on the porch.

"You look good," he admitted gruffly. And she did. Her five-foot-six-inch form was lithe and fit, her dark hair professionally cut and styled. Makeup perfect. She was dressed in a custom Western shirt and jeans, fancy boots.

Desiree drew a breath. Kept her eyes on his. Looking every bit as apprehensive as he felt. "Thanks," she said tentatively. "So do you."

Another awkward silence fell.

She reached into an expensive-looking leather carryall. "I came to invite you both to a performance I'm giving in Dallas tomorrow evening. The club is in Deep Elum." She handed over a flyer with all the information.

Cooper read out loud. "'Country Road Records presents'?"

His sister smiled proudly. "It's my official debut as one of their new artists. I thought…*hoped*, anyway…you'd want to be there."

Cooper didn't know a lot about the music industry, but he knew enough to realize that this was a very big deal. "Wow."

"You did it!" Beside him, Jillian smiled her best wishes, too.

Desire smiled shyly back. "It's just the beginning."

"A beginning you should be very proud of," Jillian confirmed.

Desiree looked at him again. Knowing heartfelt praise was not just expected, but deserved, Cooper rose and enveloped his little sister in an awkward hug she didn't quite return.

Once again, he felt he had fallen far short of what she wanted and needed from him. That in some way, he'd let his family down. He stepped back, gut clenching. "Congratulations," he said lamely.

"So you'll come?" Desiree rose, too. Promising, almost as an afterthought, "We can talk about what's going to happen next, after the show."

Aware it was late and she had to be tired after traveling, if she had come from Nashville, or even Dallas, as he expected she had, Cooper accompanied her to the edge of the porch. "You don't want to do it now?"

Just like that, a familiar wall went up. Desiree crossed her arms in front of her chest, her expression defensive. "I'd prefer you see me perform first."

Maybe it would be best to take this one step at a time, he thought, catching Jillian's wordless look, that seemed to convey he should give his sister room... Figuring Jillian knew more about how to deal with prickly women than he did, he nodded.

"Yes. Of course," he said. In the meantime, there was something even more important to address. The triplets she had to have been missing dearly, and probably wanted to see, even if she hadn't yet come out and admitted it. He inclined his head toward the second floor of the Victorian farmhouse. "The kids are asleep upstairs…"

"But of course we'll wake them if you want," Jillian added hastily, coming to stand next to Cooper.

"No." Desiree shook her head.

In three decisive strides, she was down the steps, on the sidewalk. Her back was stiff, her chin high.

"I have to go to back to Dallas tonight—we're filming a short sequence there for one of my music videos early tomorrow morning."

Without warning, Cooper's throat ached. "Do you want me to go to that, too?" he asked, watching her swiftly retreating form. He felt like he should do something.

"No," Desiree said with resounding certainty. She whirled to face him briefly. Sorrow came and went in her eyes. "Just the performance tomorrow night. I'll text you the rest of the details." She climbed into the back of the limo, and seconds later was gone.

Jillian stood next to Cooper, watching as the limo turned onto the country road and the taillights faded.

She was shaken to the core by what had just occurred. She could not imagine how he felt.

The front door opened.

Emma walked out, keys in hand, carryall bag with sketchpad looped on her shoulder. "If you-all don't need me, I'm going to give you your privacy and head on over to Mom and Dad's."

Where she was currently staying.

Needing a hug, and not sure it was the right time to approach Cooper for one, Jillian embraced her sister.

"I'm here for whatever," Emma whispered in her ear, hugging her back tightly.

Suddenly too choked up to speak, Jillian nodded. In that instant so grateful she had a family she could depend on, to be there for her.

Emma headed off.

Cooper and Jillian walked inside.

Upstairs, the house was quiet, which meant the kids were still asleep. King was dozing in front of the fireplace, his head on his paws.

Jillian put the wicker basket that had held their dinner away. "Are you okay?" she asked Cooper, coming back to him.

He was sitting at the island, elbows on the counter, head in hands. The brooding expression on his face intensified. "I can't believe she didn't at least want to look in on the girls..." he muttered, clearly heart-broken.

Nor could Jillian, if she were truthful.

But wanting to give his sister the benefit of the doubt, she sat down next to Cooper and rubbed the tense muscles in his broad shoulders consolingly. "Maybe it was easier for her to wait. Until after her show in Dallas when she could actually spend some time with them."

Cooper took a deep breath, his expression growing even more troubled. "I don't think that is it."

She didn't, either. But then, they still didn't have all the facts. She adopted a positive attitude. "Let's be happy for Desiree's success. Grateful that she is here and wanting to include you in her and the girls' life, after so many years apart."

"You're right." He stood, his manner every bit as set and determined as his departing sister's had been. He drew Jillian into his arms and held her close, finally giving her the comfort she needed. He pressed a kiss to the top of her head. "With time and effort," he promised her sincerely, "this can all be worked out."

Chapter Fifteen

"This suite is incredible!" Jillian gushed at five o'clock the next day as she and Cooper surveyed their accommodations in the downtown Dallas hotel. The elegantly furnished living room sported both a bar and coffee station, and was flanked by a bedroom with king-size bed on each side. One spa bath had a marble shower with multiple jets, the other a soaking tub big enough for two. "Your sister really did right by us."

Desiree had texted them the reservations early that morning. Or, Jillian corrected herself silently, the administrative assistant assigned to Desiree by the Country Road record label had.

His expression thoughtful, Cooper murmured,

"It *is* impressive." He turned to her, already moving on. "Think we should check in with your folks?" he asked, evidencing the same unprecedented apprehension she'd been feeling all afternoon.

Carol and Robert were staying over at Jillian's place to care for the triplets in their absence.

They'd been gone less than four hours and had already checked in twice. It would have been comical had Jillian not been experiencing the same unfounded anxiety.

Knowing there was only one thing that would put them both at ease, she pulled her phone out and sent her mom a FaceTime request. To her relief, her mom picked up immediately. She was sitting on the floor, surrounded by the triplets, who appeared to be working together to create a toy block building in the middle of the rug. "Hi, honey!" Carol said, looking happy as could be. Which wasn't surprising. She was always in her element when surrounded by children.

Her dad came into the picture. He had an apron on, which meant he was preparing dinner. He smiled. "Did you all make it there okay?"

"We did!" Jillian replied. As thrilled and relieved as Cooper appeared to be to see the triplets were indeed doing just fine without them.

"What time is Desiree singing tonight?" her mom asked.

"Ten thirty," Cooper stated with unmistakable pride. "She's the second act or main attraction."

Which was again, Jillian thought, a big deal.

"I don't know if it will be allowed, intellectual property and copyright laws and all that," her mom said, "but if it is, would you record it on your phone for us? At least a little bit. We'd love to see it."

"I will," Jillian promised.

Cooper had been watching the girls play over her shoulder. Now he stepped fully into view. "Thanks again for babysitting for us, especially on such short notice," he said.

"No problem," Carol retorted gleefully. "Now you-all just enjoy yourselves this evening, you hear? Because nights like this don't come along every day!"

"My mom is right about that," Jillian said after she had ended the call. She turned to Cooper, reveling in how good he looked, even in rumpled travel clothes, a hint of beard rimming his face. "So, what do you want to do?" she asked, feeling fancy free and over the moon excited to be with him. She tipped her head up to his. "Explore the city a bit? Go out to dinner?"

"First, this…" Coop told her huskily, taking her all the way in his arms and kissing her until her abdomen felt liquid and weightless and her knees grew weak. He brought her against him, length to length. "And then—" still kissing her ardently, he undid the buttons on her blouse and undid the clasp on her bra "—room service later…"

She took him by the hand and led him into the master bathroom, which was stocked with plenty of thick, fluffy towels, two spa robes, and an array of lotions, soaps and bubble bath.

Impulsively, she turned to face him. "I'd like a nice long soak in that big sunken tub. Care to join me?"

He caught her against him for another tantalizing kiss that had her heart racing. Then he drew back, his eyes dark and intent.

"Absolutely." He kissed her again. "Just let me get what we need from my suitcase."

Jillian started the water and put in a generous amount of fragrant bubble bath. She had just stripped down and slipped into the chest-high bubbles when Cooper strolled back in with his usual innate grace. He set the condoms next to the tub and dispensed with his clothes in a swift, purposeful way that left her mouth dry.

Like her, he was already physically, visibly aroused. She flashed him her most provocative smile. "Come on in, handsome. There's plenty of room…"

He tipped an imaginary hat, seeming as excited as she was. "Thank you, sweetheart." He winked. "Don't mind if I do."

She was trembling as he settled opposite her, took the back of her hand and kissed the tender underside of her wrist. Loving the warm, masculine feel of his lips on her skin, she gave him her most come-hither look. "In the mood for a little hot hotel sex?" she teased playfully.

"Among other things." He tugged her close. Kissing her deeply. Passionately. "But mostly," he said, cupping her face in his hands, "in the mood to be close to you. As close as possible, actually…"

Jillian sighed. Making love with Cooper was so much better than she ever could have imagined it would be. Pulse accelerating, she told him, "I think that can be arranged, cowboy…"

Trapping him right where she wanted him, she settled on his lap, her arms encircling his shoulders, her thighs pressed tight on either side of his. She gasped in pleasure when the tip of his manhood pressed against her. Then his palms moved slowly, lovingly up over her ribs. She fit her lips to his, opening her mouth, caressing his tongue, savoring the hot male taste of him. Relishing his tenderness…his strength. Finding the kind of sweet solace she had yearned for forever…

Aware that she had never felt as free and feminine and empowered as she did with him, she put her hand between them, cupping the hard velvety length of him in her palm. He groaned as she stroked, his unbridled passion fueling her own heady desire. Every part of her reveling in the heat of him, in her ability to entice him…

Jillian's nipples tingled as he bent and kissed her breasts. She moaned as his hand drifted lower still. Finding the center of her, just as she had found him. This was torture. Sweet torture. But torture nevertheless. She shifted wantonly against him, demonstrating her need, kissing him again, deeply and provocatively. "I want you now," she whispered against his mouth, reaching for the condom, rolling it on him.

Gripping her buttocks with one hand, he spread her thighs all the wider. "Not yet…" Refusing to let her rush, he caressed her inner thighs, exploring the soft curls, the soft petals within. She shuddered and gasped as he sent her libido into overdrive.

And still he kissed and touched and stroked her, with maddeningly slow intensity, until her body pulsed, her blood flowed through her veins like liquid fire and she trembled with exploding desire.

"Now," she whispered again.

"Now…" he agreed. Lifting her slightly and then bringing her down overtop of him. Pushing into her, deep. Then slow, and hard, and easy. Knowing exactly what she needed and wanted. Possessing her on his terms, even as he gave her everything, and she blissfully gave him everything in return.

They surged together, finding a solace so deep and profound it seemed impossible.

Until at last his control faltered, too. Pleasure reigned. And Jillian knew, maybe this wasn't just a short term friends-with-benefits arrangement after all.

Maybe this was a love affair that would last forever.

All she had to do was open up her heart and take a risk, and maybe Cooper would, too. And they'd finally have the full, satisfying life they both wanted.

* * *

"You're looking absolutely ravishing tonight," Cooper said as they headed down to the front entrance, where a car, ordered by Desiree's label, waited to take them to the venue. He cast an appreciative look at her silver sheath dress and heels.

"You're looking really hot, too." Admiring his tall, handsome form, Jillian placed her hand in his.

They moved through the lobby, found their ride. "Is it crazy for me to be so nervous for Desiree?" he asked, sliding in the back of the town car after her.

Aware this was what it would be like if they were actually a real couple, Jillian cuddled against him and tenderly stroked his jaw. He had shaved and put on that spicy wintergreen cologne she loved. "I'm nervous, too. I really want it to go well for her."

Their gazes locked and she felt another moment of tingling awareness. The kind that happened when you were on the brink of falling in love...

Cooper kissed her. "Me, too."

Short minutes later, the driver pulled up to let them out. The club in Deep Elum was packed with patrons. People also queued up outside. They wouldn't have gotten in had they not had special passes.

Listening to the warm-up band, which was awfully good, too, Jillian could only imagine the depth of talent Desiree was going to display.

To her joy, she wasn't disappointed.

The woman had a voice that was both compelling and soothing, emotional and memorable.

Desiree went through all the songs on her upcoming album. From the toe-tapping girl gone wild ditty, to the brokenhearted lament of a woman who had been left.

But it was the last song she sang, accompanied only by her acoustic guitar, that seemed to really say it all.

It was called "Burden." She sang it straight to Cooper.

"I never wanted to be your burden. No…
I know I let you down.
But I've got mountains to climb.
And staying home is just wasted time…
I tried everything I could to make you let me go…
To give you your freedom, and your own life back…
You refused…
Said I was your duty…
But all I felt was the terrible burden I was to you…
The burden I was to you…
Maybe you'll understand one day.
And we'll be able to love each other again.
At least that is my hope.
Because I can't take your judgment…the feeling that even now I've wronged and disappointed you…

Disappointed you…
Just by being me.
And wanting and needing the things I want
and need…
Yes, I can do it on my own.
But I want you, need you, on my side…
Need you to hear me. See me. Not for who I
was, but who I am. And all I aspire to be.
Ohhhhhhh…
Let's finally put the past aside, and be more
than family that no longer speaks.
Because I never wanted to be your burden.
Never wanted to let you down…"

The song ended on a mournful note. Tears were streaming down Jillian's face. Cooper's eyes were glistening, too.

The crowd erupted in wild applause. Desiree slipped off the stool she had been sitting on and stood, taking a bow, her face shining with happiness in the light of the stage. And Jillian knew, even if Cooper had yet to admit it, that this was where his sister deserved to be.

Two encores and many rounds of applause later, Jillian, Desiree, the label executive managing her debut and Cooper were finally in the limo sent to collect them. Headed for the luxurious downtown hotel where they were all staying.

"So, what did you think?" Desiree asked when

the three of them were finally alone in her penthouse suite on the very top floor of the hotel. Room service had delivered a late-night supper, along with a bottle of expensive champagne.

"Incredible," Cooper said sincerely. "And that last song…" He choked up, unable to go on.

Jillian found herself inundated with emotion, as well.

Desiree sat at the table, gesturing for them to join her. She fixed herself a plate of food. They did the same. "It's new. I wrote it a few days ago." The expression on her face was calm but wary. "When I was thinking about the conversation we were going to have. What I was going to have to ask you."

Jillian had a funny feeling this was not going to be good.

"I'm listening," Cooper said soberly.

Desiree squared her slender shoulders and took a deep breath. "I want you to become the girls' legal guardian and adopt them, Coop. Raise them as your own."

The whole world seemed to stop.

Cooper went still. He stared at his sister as if she had grown two heads. "You're giving them up?" he asked hoarsely, blinking in disbelief.

Desiree met his even glance with remarkable composure. "Yes."

He pushed away from the table, stood and began to pace. "I can't… It's a mistake."

Desiree remained where she was and put a napkin

on her lap. "The mistake would be in trying to keep them and have the kind of superstardom I want."

Cooper came back to the table and sat down.

Jillian felt like she was watching a slow-motion train wreck. Helpless to do anything about it...

He leaned toward his sister. "There has to be a middle ground," he insisted urgently.

Desiree shook her head. Looking tired now. Resigned. "No, Coop, there isn't. I signed a multiyear contract with the Country Roads record label. It requires me to put out at least one album every twelve months. Make music videos. Do promotion everywhere and anywhere they say. And play whatever concert venues they set up." She sighed. "Right now they will all be small, as they try to get me known, but eventually they'd like to see me filling stadiums. All that comes with a cost. I'm not going to have a personal life or time for anything but work. And I certainly won't have time to be mother to three beautiful babies who deserve so much more than I can give them."

Cooper regarded her empathetically. "I know you feel pressure now, trying to get everything done, but there will come a day when you will be glad you didn't give up on your family to pursue a career."

Jillian pivoted to stare at him. She knew Cooper had his family's best interests at heart, but he was presuming an awful lot. Desiree thought so, too. She glared at him.

"So what are you saying? You don't want to assume custody of the kids?"

Grimacing, he told her, "I'm saying I'm not going to tell you that it's okay for you to make the biggest mistake of your life."

Desiree went white, then red. She regarded her brother stoically. "This is happening, Cooper, whether you agree with my decision or not." Desiree turned to Jillian. "What about you? I know you love the triplets and have taken wonderful care of them in my absence. Every photo and text you've sent me has shown me that."

Glad her efforts had reaped some benefit, Jillian sent her a sympathetic glance and said quietly, "I wanted you to know they were okay."

Some of the fight went out of Desiree. Her posture relaxed. "And it helped me, *believe me*, to know there really could be a better situation for them." She dragged a fork through her thus far untouched food. Looked up. Drew another deep, enervating breath. "So." She looked Jillian in the eye. "Are you interested in becoming their guardian and raising them as your own?"

"I'll take care of them however, whenever you need me to," Jillian promised.

Desiree exhaled, suddenly looking as miserable as Cooper did. Briefly, she shut her eyes. "It's okay if you decide it's too much." She swallowed. "There are several other prospective parents lined up, ready to step in, if you can't."

Give the triplets to strangers to raise?

Absolutely not!

Not when they already had another home where they were loved and cherished!

Jillian reached across the table and took both Desiree's hands in hers. "It's not too much," she said fiercely, knowing it was true from the depths of her soul. "I want them." *Cooper wants them, too, even if he is too distraught right now to admit it.*

Desiree studied her. "You're sure?"

"Yes," Jillian said emphatically, ignoring the irked and astonished look that Cooper was giving her.

Finally, Desiree produced a small smile of gratitude and relief. She retrieved her bag and produced a card. "This is my attorney. He is going to handle the details of the private adoption."

"At least see the girls again," Cooper implored. "Before you make a decision this monumental."

Desiree shook her head mulishly, digging in every bit as much as her brother. "I said my goodbye when I made my decision last month."

"Don't. Do. This," Cooper said raggedly.

Finally, Desiree's eyes filled with tears. "Don't you…do this to me…" she said brokenly.

And in that moment, Jillian knew, there wasn't a heart in the room that wasn't shattered to pieces.

Chapter Sixteen

Jillian and Cooper walked in silence to the elevator that would take them to their floor. And from there, the hall to their own suite.

Cooper shut the door behind them. Then took off his sport coat and walked to the window, looking out on the sparkling city lights.

Jillian stepped out of her heels and joined him at the window. A tidal wave of emotion swirling through her, she curved a hand over his biceps. He had never seemed so aloof. She understood the shock he had been through. She felt it, too. She also suspected he was so blinded by hurt and pain that he couldn't see things any other way than his own point of view right now.

Telling herself it wasn't too late to get through to him, to help him see reason and keep his family from being ripped apart all the more, she swallowed hard around the lump in her throat. "What are you thinking?"

He turned to her, regarding her like she had purposefully betrayed him. "What was Desiree talking about when she said you had been texting her?"

Aware her heart had been in the right place, Jillian pushed away the dagger edge of guilt. "I texted her little photos and updates on the girls almost every day she was gone." There were a few days at the beginning when she hadn't. But once she had started, she had kept it up.

His jaw set. He went to the minibar and plugged in the suite coffee maker. Filled it with water and got out one of the packets. "You didn't think I had a right to know that?" he asked incredulously.

Jillian leaned against the counter, watching as he unwrapped the prefilled coffee filter with quick, economical motions, set up the brewer, then turned it on. As simply as she could, she tried to explain. "I was trying to bridge the emotional distance between you and your sister. As well as assure her that the girls were fine."

Cooper pinned her with a hard stare.

Jillian lifted her hands and persisted calmly, "Because I thought Desiree might be...*had* to be...at least a little bit anxious about how they were doing without her." She paused to search Cooper's eyes.

"The same way you and I were worried tonight when we got to the hotel. Given the fact it was the first time either of us had been more than five or ten minutes away from them."

As the smell of fresh-brewed coffee filled the suite, he lounged opposite her, forearms braced on the bar top. "I would've liked to know if she was in touch with you." Hurt laced his low tone. "Especially since she wasn't responding at all to me."

Jillian closed the distance between them. "I'm sorry. I didn't tell you because I didn't want you to be hurt, because…" She splayed her palms over the warm, hard surface of his chest and tipped her face up to his. "She didn't respond at all to me, either," she admitted, aware Cooper was making no effort to embrace her. Or touch her in any way.

Getting the message, Jillian dropped her hands. Stepped back. Continuing contritely. "I mean, I put a Read Receipt on every message so I knew she was opening them."

Cooper seemed to take little comfort from that.

Drawing a deep bolstering breath, Jillian shoved a hand through her hair and pushed on. "Had Desiree actually written back or liked a text or done anything like that at all, *I would have told you immediately.*"

Aware the minibrew was finished, Cooper turned and filled two mugs. He handed her one. "But she didn't."

"No." While he drank his black, she added sugar and creamer packets to hers. Then used a plastic stirrer to swirl it in. She lifted the cup to her lips and took a sip of the slightly acidic brew. Still holding the cup between her hands, she continued looking at him. "But I kept trying," she admitted emotionally, "because I do believe with love all things are possible."

His handsome features were etched with bitterness. "The only problem is she doesn't love her daughters."

Beneath the disillusionment in his low tone was something else. Something nearly as unsettling. "That's not the impression I got," Jillian countered, her own heart swelling with compassion and love. For Cooper. The girls. And especially Desiree. Who was obviously struggling so hard to do the right thing. And deep down she knew that this had to be tearing his sister apart, even as it set her free…

Cooper stared at her, as if she were a stranger. "Desiree is giving them up."

Jillian knew that. It wasn't a choice she could or would ever make herself. But she wasn't Desiree. She didn't have her depth of talent, or her overwhelming need to share that incredible gift with the world.

"Because she wants a better life for them than she is going to be able to provide."

Cooper paused, his brow furrowed. "She'll have money now. Which means she can afford all sorts of very qualified help."

"But she won't be there for them." Aware she suddenly felt so shaky she could barely stand, Jillian put her own barely touched beverage aside. She tucked her arms against her chest to still their trembling. "She's going to be working and traveling. Performing constantly."

"Which is another thing." He quaffed the rest of his coffee and set the cup down with a thud. Looking completely outraged, he demanded, "What kind of person puts their career above their kids?"

Jillian straightened to her full height. "Ah…every person who has an extremely high-level job that requires them to give one hundred and ten percent of their life to their job every single day."

He kept his dark gaze locked with hers. "Most of them have spouses or other family to assist in the care of any children."

Exactly! "Which is where you—and I—" she interjected herself because she knew he would need her as much as the girls would "—step in, Coop."

"Except Desiree is not asking us to continue babysitting, Jillian. She wants one or both of us to assume full custody and guardianship."

Empathy swelled in Jillian's heart, mixing with the confusion she felt. She and Cooper were so close in so many ways. Why weren't they on the same page here, too? Was something else really happening here? Something she didn't want to see…?

"Which has to be even harder on Desiree's end of things," she insisted.

Cooper paced the suite restlessly. "I can't help

my sister make a mistake that she will regret the rest of her life."

Jillian knit her hands together in front of her. Still struggling to understand where he was coming from, she pushed on. "So, you're saying *you* know what's best for her, better than Desiree does?"

"I do."

Jillian looked him right in the eye, reminding him quietly, "The way you did when she asked you to donate some of her belongings to the charity that helped other single moms? And instead, you took them to your ranch because you were sure the Nashville thing wasn't going to work out, after all, and Desiree was going to need them later?"

His expression tautened. "She still might."

"Coop." It was all Jillian could do to keep her voice from rising. "Didn't you listen to that song she sang? 'Burden.' Didn't you watch her light up on stage tonight, or see how every single person in the audience related to her? She is a *phenomenal* talent. In fact, I think, given her incredibly beautiful distinctive voice and songwriting skills, that she may very well be the next Miranda Lambert!"

Cooper stared at Jillian in weary resignation, then spread his hands wide, reminding her curtly, "I don't disagree with that."

She stepped closer. "Do you want her to have everything she deserves?"

"Absolutely."

"Then…?"

"She still shouldn't have to choose between stardom and her kids."

"It's *her* life, Cooper. Her decision to make. Not yours or mine, or anyone else's. Only she knows what is right for her."

Silence fell between them.

"I still can't make it easy on her, or help her make a decision that I know she'll regret the rest of her life. Her kids, too, maybe."

Jillian knew Cooper loved Sadie, Tess and Hallie every bit as much as she did. That he thought he was doing the right thing. Even if it was wrong.

"Let me ask you something," Jillian said eventually, still determined to get through to him. "If this weren't about her work. If instead," she continued thickly, "you had received word tonight that your sister had passed due to some dreadful accident or disease…and she had named you the triplets' guardian, would you do it?"

He stood stone-still. "That's not what happened."

She wished they could call a time-out on all of this and fall into each other's arms and make love, and let all their problems fade away, but she also knew that would only be avoiding the inevitable.

Taking in the set of his broad shoulders and the taut muscles of his chest, she said, "Answer the question."

"Of course, I would."

"Then why are you so resistant to doing it now?" She put up a staying hand, took a deep breath and frowned. "And don't tell me it's because you disapprove of her decision." Because the excessively judgmental man in front of her was not the Cooper she knew and admired. Or the person who had jumped in without a qualm and taken such loving care of his nieces for the past month.

"There has to be something more causing you to react so emotionally," she persisted doggedly. Something that had pushed his buttons and set off a firestorm of emotion and doubt within him.

She stepped closer still. "What is it?"

Leave it to Jillian to be able to dig deep enough, to see into the dark recesses of his heart. Figuring he might as well confide in someone, Cooper told her the real reason he couldn't take on the triplets. "Because I'm the reason Desiree's failing as a mother," he said gruffly. "It's my fault."

She took his hand and led him over to the sofa. "How do you figure that?" She urged him to sit beside her.

Reluctantly, Cooper did. "My sister was fine until my parents passed and I insisted on marrying Linda and taking guardianship of Desiree. And then she went from the most loving and sensitive kid sister I ever could have wished for to someone who was completely and utterly selfish and self-involved. She didn't care what effect her actions had on anyone else, or who she hurt. Desiree wanted what she wanted and that was that."

"Don't you think all abruptly orphaned kids feel that way to some extent? I mean… I know *I* did. I felt the only person who could take care of me was me, and I was hurting so bad, and felt so alone, I didn't have the energy to care about anyone else. That soul-deep loneliness is what made me so susceptible to Chip Harcourt's lies. His romantic promises to protect me the way no one else ever had.

Jillian paused and drew a breath. "Don't you see, Coop?" She stared into his eyes, begging him to understand, in a way that disappointed almost as much as his sister's selfishness. "It's more than Desiree being too involved with her rocker boyfriend at the time. It's about the way she lost the ability to connect with or really honor family."

Cooper rubbed his palm on his leg in frustration. Jillian was trying to give him a pass when he did not deserve one. "None of that would have happened if my parents had lived," he reminded her grimly, "so obviously, I did something wrong." Much as he would have liked to, he could not walk away from that.

She swung toward him in exasperation. "Are you talking about the fact you made Desiree feel like a burden?"

That was not only right on target but stung almost as much as the heart-rending lyrics his sister had sung to him. He countered brusquely, "I mean because I didn't know the first thing about being a parent." Maybe, given the way he was at such a loss, he still didn't. A muscle ticked in his jaw. "Or, I *don't* know. Maybe I just don't have what it takes to shepherd a traumatized child into an emotionally healthy adult." Never mind convince his sister not to ruin her and her children's lives.

Jillian made a face that indicated that wasn't it. "The triplets aren't traumatized, Coop."

He paused, aware she seemed sort of skeptical. "Because of all the extra people, like Darcy and her girls, and the volunteers—" he countered.

She threw up her hands. "And us!"

"—around them. Loving them," he concluded.

Jillian drew back and searched his eyes. "These are remarkably well-adjusted babies, Coop. They eat and laugh and play and hug and sleep through the night." Her sea-blue eyes gleamed passionately. "And that would *not* be happening if Desiree hadn't loved them dearly, too."

Disappointment turned to a sorrow that burrowed into the depths of his soul. Once again, he had failed his only sibling. "Just not enough to make them the main priority in her life."

Jillian took his hand and clasped it warmly. "Luckily, your sister and the girls have us. Because we have been doing just that and will continue to do so."

Cooper withdrew his hand from the soft comfort of hers. Though he wanted nothing more than to haul Jillian into his arms and make hot wild love to her, he wouldn't, because he wanted more than sex and friendship between them. He wanted them to be able to talk honestly, and support each other completely, even when they bitterly disagreed. And right now, he needed her on his side.

"I meant what I said to my sister, Jillian. I won't make this easy for her. Or let her run away from family again. Or help her make the biggest mistake of her life."

Stunned, Jillian raked her teeth across her lusciously soft lower lip. "You really mean that."

"Yes." He leaned forward eagerly, presenting his solution. "If you and I refuse to take the kids, then Desiree's going to have to stop and think—"

Jillian rose, her spine rigid. Her patience apparently at an end, she stared down at him angrily. "No, Coop. If you and I both refuse, Desiree will simply call her lawyer, and the girls will be put in yet another unfamiliar situation. One that you and I will have no control over. And I am *not* going to let that happen. Not after what I've been through," she continued in a broken-sounding tone. "And not when I already love them with all my heart and soul."

He knew that.

And yet…

"You've said for years you didn't want marriage or kids, that you were happy being a single aunt…"

"Well, I was wrong. If the last month has shown me anything, it's that I do want both those things."

Part of him felt that way, too. The last month had been so full of love and laughter and fun times; he often found himself wondering how he was going to manage without Jillian and the triplets. And how crazy was that, given he'd erased all romance from his life and never been a baby person? "There are *three* girls, Jillian," he reminded her reasonably. "They need more than one parent."

"So?" she said quietly, the determination he loved about her resurging. "Step up and share permanent custody with me, then."

His heart wrenched in his chest. "We're not married."

"So?" She waved a hand, as if it were just an obstacle meant to be shoved aside, and glided close enough he could inhale her delicate feminine perfume. "We could easily rectify that."

She was *proposing* to him? How reckless of heart was she prepared to be? "You mean enter into a marriage of convenience?" he asked, stunned.

"Well, it wouldn't be a marriage of convenience to me," she admitted reluctantly as hurt flickered across her face, then disappeared altogether. "But if you prefer to think of it that way, then fine, it can be more of a modern-day 'familial arrangement' than a traditional marriage," she conceded, gathering steam.

Cooper remembered how much he had hurt his first wife and his sister, how he had fooled himself by pretending that everything would all work out.

Determined to avoid the same trap when the romance faded and the reality of it all set in, he forced himself to be ruthlessly practical this time. Putting his feelings aside, he said tersely, "Well, the reality is, a hasty marriage between us would be more of a means to an end than anything else." And that, he knew in his gut, was wrong.

She would realize it, too, if she would take her emotions out of the situation!

Jillian threw up her hands and began to pace. "Fine then," she said, sighing, "let's stay single. And continue being friends with benefits. It doesn't really matter what our formal legal status is, as long as the girls have a 'mommy' and a 'daddy' in their life," she reiterated passionately. "And we have been and could still be that."

Her life-is-nothing-but-a-fairy-tale attitude rankled. He stood to square off with her. "I went down this road before with Linda, remember?" he reminded her as they went toe-to-toe. It had been an unmitigated disaster. "When the honeymoon period fades…we'll end up with nothing but regrets. And our eventual breakup will hurt the girls the same way Desiree was hurt." He couldn't bear that.

Staring up at him, she balled her hands into fists at her sides and countered in a low, achingly vulnerable voice. "You're so sure we would end up divorced?"

He didn't want to think that way. But he couldn't afford to be as starry-eyed and idealistic as Jillian was being. Not with all six of their hearts and lives at stake.

"If we rush into something like this for all the wrong reasons, then yes, I am." He touched her shoulder lightly. "Which is why we need to take a step back and stop reacting so impulsively."

Her expression closed. She moved away. "You mean find another family to take the triplets?"

It killed him to even think about it, but...he had to put the children's welfare first. Not Jillian's. Not his own. "If Desiree doesn't come to her senses, yes. That probably would be best for them," he admitted reluctantly. Even if it would break his and Jillian's hearts. "Because at the end of the day, I want them to have the kind of stable, normal childhood my sister and I had before our parents passed. The kind you had when Carol and Robert adopted you and your siblings." A family supported by a foundation of everlasting love and commitment. Not one cobbled together as a practical solution.

Her eyes were serious and searching. "And you don't think you and I can give them that?"

Aching at the susceptibility he saw in her face, he admitted reluctantly, "As great as it's been, hanging out together, all we've been doing is enjoying an extended babysitting gig. And playing house."

She reeled as if absorbing a physical blow. "Really." Hurt and anger flared in her eyes. "That's *all* it's felt like to you? *Playing house?*"

Damn it, what was wrong with him? Why couldn't he communicate effectively tonight? How come he was pushing her away when all he wanted was to draw her close? Feeling like he needed Jillian more than ever, he put up a hand, amending hastily,

"That doesn't mean we can't or won't have more over time. If we go back to the beginning and are together strictly because we want to be, not just because we're more or less forced to be, in order to care for the kids." He spread his hands wide in a placating gesture. "Once Desiree comes to her senses and agrees to do what is right by her children—" *which she surely would if Jillian helped him persuade his sister* "—this could be a whole new start for you and me." *One that could end happily for all.*

Unfortunately, he wasn't sure Jillian was in agreement with that, as another tense silence ensued. She stared at him as if he had lost all compassion. Finally, she shook her head. Stepped away. "You're right, Cooper." Her back to him, she declared, "The triplets do deserve *a lot more* than you will ever be able to give them."

Finally, he thought on a sigh of relief, she understood!

Jillian squared her slender shoulders, let out a long, beleaguered breath. She looked him right in the eye and said with steely resolve, "Which is why I am going to continue on with this adoption on my own."

Wait. What?

She swiftly packed up her belongings, snapped the closures on her overnight bag and headed for the exit.

Aware now his world really was crashing down around him, he stopped her at the door. "You're reacting as recklessly as Desiree." For the life of him, he couldn't understand why.

Her hand still on the doorknob, she swung on him and explained with stinging disappointment, "No, Coop, I'm following my heart on the only path that will generate love."

A mutual sorrow engulfed them.

"It's too bad you're too stubborn and closed off to be able to do the same thing," she said sadly. After another long, disappointed look, she walked out.

Chapter Seventeen

Two weeks later...

"So how did it go with the attorney?" Faith asked as soon as they had gotten the triplets and baby Quinn asleep for the night.

Glad her sister had come over to spend the night and indulge in a little girl talk, Jillian set out a tray of snacks and opened a bottle of wine. "Good. Because it is an independent adoption between two private parties, and we are essentially family friends, it's going to be a lot simpler than I expected." They settled on the sofa.

Faith munched on a slice of cheddar. "How is Desiree doing?"

Jillian sipped her wine. "Better, now that she has terminated her parental rights."

Faith frowned. "I would've thought the opposite would be true."

"I know." She sighed. "Me, too."

"Have the two of you been communicating directly? Or is everything just through the lawyers?"

Aware how empty the house had been since Cooper had moved back to Rock Creek, Jillian admitted, "Desiree and I have been talking. A lot, actually. After Cooper reacted the way he did, I had to make sure that I really was supporting his sister the way I thought I was, that I wasn't just taking the easy path and encouraging her to make a mistake."

Faith listened intently. "And you're sure?"

Jillian nodded. At peace about this much. "Desiree told me she had suspicions from the very beginning that she wasn't cut out to be a mom. But she had the triplets anyway, and told herself she would give it one year. To be sure."

"It wasn't just a matter of her feeling overwhelmed by the physical and emotional demands of caring for three babies simultaneously?"

Jillian shook her head. "She said Darcy and her teenage daughters helped her out a lot. Along with the nearby church day care that waived the tuition for the girls. Otherwise, she probably wouldn't have made it. But she was always able to do the basic things that needed to be done. Like feeding them, and changing their diapers, getting them on a schedule and singing them to sleep," Jillian recollected. "But she also said she resented the time they took away from her music. That it was the music inside her that kept her going, and the triplets kept her from fully devoting herself to her art, and or realizing her potential."

"Desiree must have really felt torn," Faith empathized.

"She really did. She told me she was alive on stage. At home, she was just marking time until she could get the triplets down for a nap and get back to her songwriting." Jillian shook her head sadly. "And she knew that was no way to live. No way for the girls to grow up. And that it was a situation that would only grow worse over time."

"How does she feel now?" Faith asked.

"She is at peace about giving them up to me to raise. Because she knows that I love them and will do right by them."

Faith's glance turned to the framed photos of the triplets that Jillian had put up on the mantel. "Is she going to be involved in their life at all?"

Jillian shook her head. "Right now she is saying no. But we left the door open, so that at any time in the future, she will be able to see them. But as their aunt, not as their biological mother. In the meantime, I am going to send updates to a private email address we set up, so that if she wants to know they are okay, she can check and see. And if she doesn't look, that will be all right, too."

Faith sipped her wine. "Sounds like you two really worked this all out."

"We did." Jillian munched on a cracker.

"You seem to really like her."

"I do," Jillian admitted candidly. "She's one of the most emotionally honest and self-aware people I've ever met."

Remembering she still had a load of baby clothes to fold, Jillian went to get the laundry basket and set it between them.

"What about Cooper and their relationship?" Faith helped her fold.

Jillian sorted the pajamas from the dresses and put them in stacks. "Not surprisingly, it's totally on the rocks. And his sister is still disappointed about that, the fact that the two of them stopped talking again. But she wasn't really surprised." Jillian matched socks. "She said he never listened to her when she tried to tell him what she wanted or needed to be happy."

Faith lifted a brow. "It sounds like he didn't listen to you, either."

So true. Wishing she had more chores to do, because sitting led to thinking…and thinking led to feeling…and right now the only thing she wanted to feel was her happiness about adopting three baby girls. *Not* the heartbreak that was tearing her up inside at losing Cooper. Swallowing past the lump in her throat, Jillian put the neatly folded stacks back into the basket. "It doesn't really matter."

"Are you sure about that? Because it doesn't look to me like you're the least bit over him."

She wasn't. And at this point, she didn't think she ever would be.

Jillian carried the basket to the foot of the stairs, to take up later. "That doesn't matter, either."

Faith studied her. "Hmm. Well…"

And here it comes. The advice I don't want to receive…

Faith waited for Jillian to rejoin her on the sofa. "What I don't understand is why you are being as stubborn about all this as Cooper is."

Jillian huffed. "What do you mean?"

Much more empathetic, since she had lost her military-vet husband in a construction accident earlier in the year, Faith asked kindly, "Why won't you give Cooper the time he seems to need to come to the same conclusion you already have, that the triplets belong with both of you?"

Jillian's heart ached. "Because he's never going to get there."

"Because he didn't love the triplets enough after all," Faith surmised sadly.

Jillian straightened. "Of course he loves them!" she corrected her sister indignantly. "It's Cooper's fierce need to nurture and protect the girls that made him take such a hard stance with his sister in the first place!"

Faith squinted. "You don't think that could change over time?"

She wanted it to! So badly!

Jillian waved an airy hand. "It's really a moot point, now. He opted out of all of our lives when he refused to honor his sister and me, and listen to what either of us said… and follow what I know darn well was in his heart."

"Which was what?" her sister asked.

"To assume permanent care of his nieces—with me."

Faith was motionless. "Wait a minute. I thought he wanted to start over with you, if the triplets stayed with Desiree."

Jillian was suddenly on the verge of tears. "Exactly. He wanted to be with me if certain conditions were met," she recounted bitterly. "If they weren't, then he wasn't interested. And I can't go there, Faith. I can't go backward. Not when I finally opened myself up to the possibility of love and family again…" Even if, she thought ironically, she had foolishly followed her feelings and opened her heart up to a man who couldn't fully open up his!

Faith lifted a censuring brow. "Well, if your heart is truly open," she countered sagely, "then there ought to be room for Cooper, even if what he can offer you right now isn't exactly what you want, either."

"What is it, boy? Do we have company?" Cooper asked several days later.

King cocked his head, then turned and padded toward the front door of the Rock Creek ranch house. Cooper put down his electric screwdriver and followed him out onto the front porch.

Carol Lockhart was getting out of her car, a wicker picnic basket looped over her arm. "I hope this is a good time to drop by," she said brightly.

He wasn't sure there was ever going to be a good time, given the excruciatingly abrupt way he and Jillian had ended their relationship.

Carol had been nothing but kind to him and his three nieces, though. He owed her the same courtesy. "Come in," he said. "Although I apologize in advance for the mess."

She checked out the newly drywalled first floor and the solid maple kitchen cabinets he was assembling. "Wow. You've made a lot of progress."

Cooper'd had to do something to fill up the time, now that he was no longer caring for the triplets or seeing Jillian at all. Ranch work could only occupy him so much.

Carol handed over the wicker basket, then gestured at all he had renovated. "What inspired you to pick up the pace?" she asked.

Hallie. Sadie. Tess. And *Jillian*, he thought, the ache of unwanted solitude growing by leaps and bounds.

"It was time," Cooper said succinctly. A peek inside the basket showed it to be full of a home-cooked roast beef dinner with man-size portions. He inhaled the delicious aroma. Grinned gratefully. "And thanks for the meal. It looks delicious."

"You're welcome. Although I expect you know it was only an excuse to see you." Carol bent to pet King. She slipped a dog biscuit from her pocket and gave him the treat.

Grimacing because he had an idea what was coming next, he said, "You going to tell me I'm making a mistake, too?"

Carol's eyes glowed with maternal kindness. "I would never presume to judge," she told him softly. "I know that you're doing the best you can do. That you always have."

Cooper's throat ached. He had missed having a mom. So much. Carol was the closest he'd come since his own had passed. "Thanks," he said gruffly. He went to the fridge and got out two waters.

"Do you want to talk about it?" she said gently, her dual skill as social worker and veteran mom coming into play.

Cooper's throat constricted with the effort to hold back the emotion. "I don't know what there is to say," he said hoarsely.

They sat down on the sofa that had come from his sister's apartment and was still stored at the ranch house, although she'd told him again that he could donate it.

He pulled over the big steamer trunk that had once stored the triplets' toys and done dual duty as a coffee table.

"Well, then, let me ask you this," Carol went on, undeterred. She set her water bottle on the table. "If you had to do it all over again…even knowing what you know now… Would you still ask to be Desiree's guardian, if that meant keeping her out of the foster care system, and with you?"

Cooper didn't even have to think. "Yes."

The older woman nodded, as if that was exactly what she had expected to hear from him. "If Desiree had come back after running away that first time, would you have taken her back in, tried to make things work?"

Cooper inhaled, wishing he could go back and have a do-over. "Yes." *God, yes.*

Carol frowned. "So what's different now? Why won't you give Desiree another chance to work things out, as family?"

Because he couldn't bear to fail at anything that important. Again. Which, sadly, had been exactly where they were headed. "If she wanted to work things out with us as a family, she wouldn't have surrendered all legal rights to her kids and put them up for adoption."

Carol drew back, looked Cooper in the eyes and inquired, "So it's the fact that your little sister disappointed you that has you walking away. Refusing to do as she wishes and accept guardianship of her triplets."

It was so much more than that. Cooper gestured

aimlessly. "I'm no better at parenting now than I was then," he admitted gruffly.

"So you're opting out…?"

"Yes, To prevent another catastrophe down the road."

"Well, that's one way to look at it," Carol said empathically. "Another is that it's time to give yourself a break regarding past mistakes and dig deep inside of you, and use this opportunity to be there for Desiree and support her dreams the way you've admitted that you did not do in the past."

"How?" Cooper asked, ready to listen to the older woman's advice.

"By going back to taking things one step at a time and doing what she asked of you, and becoming the father figure and legal guardian her children need again."

"Except it's too late for that," Cooper rasped.

Jillian had jumped in to go it alone, making it clear there was no longer any room for him in her or the triplets' lives.

Carol lifted an encouraging brow. "It's never too late to love someone, Cooper." She reached over to pat his hand. "And it will never be too late for you to parent Desiree's children the way you were unable to parent her, when the two of you were orphaned and you were little more than a kid yourself…"

Jillian did not know what had gotten into her two sisters. Emma and Faith had been on her case ever since they had arrived at Rosehaven an hour earlier for a sibling get-together.

"You really should do something about your hair," Emma said, surveying the messy topknot on the back of her head.

"Run a brush through it or something," Faith agreed with a frown.

"And that shirt." Emma pointed. "Did you know it has *drool* on it?"

"Yes!" Jillian sent her sister an exasperated glance. "Which is to be expected since all three of the girls are getting new teeth right now."

"Still. We're here," Faith countered, like the completely pulled together mom that she was. "You *could* tidy up a bit."

Jillian looked down at herself. So her T-shirt was old and comfortably worn. Her sneakers comfy and her denim shorts faded to a pale blue. They still had four kids to feed, if you counted Faith's foster son, Quinn, and the triplets. Plus baths and bedtime…

"How about later," she said. After they had talked and devised a plan that would enable her to win Coop back!

Emma frowned. "How about now?" she insisted.

The doorbell rang.

Faith and Emma exchanged knowing looks. "Tell me you did not fix me up with someone!" Jillian said.

"Would we do that?" they chorused innocently in unison.

Yes, she thought on an exasperated huff. They

most certainly would. All she'd heard from her entire family the past three weeks was that she needed
to do something about her broken heart. Find a way
to forgive and forget and move on. As if it were that
easy! Did they really think she could so easily replace Cooper, after the way he had taken permanent
residence in her heart?

Judging by the looks on her sisters' faces, apparently so!

Scowling in frustration, she went to the door and
swung it open. Ready to send whoever it was on his
or her merry way.

Except it was Cooper, she realized, her heart
squeezing hard.

Dressed for an evening out, in sport coat, button-
down shirt and slacks. His hair was brushed neatly
back from his forehead, his face clean-shaven and
smelling of the spicy wintergreen cologne she loved.
He had a bouquet of Texas bluebonnets in his hand.

He looked at once hopeful and wary. "Can we
talk?"

Knowing now why it had been so important she
get cleaned up, she stepped out onto the porch, closing the door behind her. If Emma and Faith had only
warned her, she would be looking as smokin' hot as
he did right now. Instead, she felt embarrassingly
messy and off-kilter. "I'm going to kill my sisters."

"Don't." He flashed a sexy smile. Taking her by
the hand, he drew her out onto the front porch, where
they could talk alone.

Cooper guided her over to the chain-hung swing and sat down beside her, shifting so they were knee to knee. "I needed their help…" he said gruffly, his expression maddeningly inscrutable. His eyes roved her head to toe, drinking her in, as thirsty for her as she was for him.

"Help for what?" Her tension building, Jillian could only stare at him.

"For getting the time alone with you that I needed," he murmured, covering her hands with his. "So I could finally take you out on that date to the Laramie Country Inn we missed."

Her breath caught in her throat.

If their time apart had taught her anything, it was that she didn't want to let differing points of view keep them apart. He had made the first move. She would make the second. "Tonight," she ascertained, her heart pounding like a wild thing in her chest.

"Yes. But first," he said, his low husky tone revealing just how much soul-searching he had been doing during their time away from each other. "I want to apologize to you properly about being wrong *about everything.* For not understanding Desiree and accepting and loving her for who she is. For refusing to take on the challenge of raising a family and adopting the triplets."

Jillian knew what it took for him to admit that. She splayed her hands across his chest, the rapid beat of his heart matching hers.

"But most of all," he rasped, his eyes gleaming

with emotion as he laid it all on the line, "I want you to know how sorry I am for not giving us a chance."

The sorrow in her heart receded even as the ache in her throat grew. "Why didn't you?"

He stared into her eyes, his expression raw and filled with the same yearning she harbored deep inside. "I didn't want to screw it up." He shook his head in regret.

She searched his face, still not knowing what lay ahead, almost afraid to wish…

Hoarsely, he admitted, "I thought I would hurt you less if I promised and expected less. When…the truth is…if you love someone, if you open up your heart to them, you are going to be hurt sometimes." He hauled in another rough breath. "The question you have to ask yourself is, is it worth it? And now that I know being cautious is not the same as being closed off, I know it is. That even when we disagree, we can and will work through it. All we have to do is try."

Relief filtered through her. She moved all the way into his arms. He felt so warm and strong and solid. "Oh, Cooper, I love you so much!" She kissed him passionately.

He drew her to her feet and kissed her back, holding her close. "I love you, too. More than words can say."

She looked up at him, luxuriating in the feel of him so close to her. He had admitted his shortcomings. It was time for her to confess hers. "But this isn't all your fault," she said, flushing beneath his tender scrutiny. "I've been scared, too. Ever since my first set of parents passed, I've been afraid of running out of time. And that's made me impulsive and reckless," she murmured softly. "It's made me not want to stop and take the opportunity to really consider things, for fear that something unexpected would happen and my life would collapse again."

She leaned her head back to better see into his eyes. The tears she'd been holding back spilled over her lashes and fell down her cheeks. Her voice caught. "But the last few weeks I've realized all you really need to succeed is love, that everything else can be worked out, given time and effort."

He regarded her soberly. "I'm ready to put that in."

She kissed the underside of his jaw, relief flowing through her. "I am, too."

He kissed her sweetly and tenderly, then drew back. "And just so you know. I flew to Nashville to see Desiree yesterday. We spent the day together and had a long heart-to-heart. It's going to be okay between us now."

Relief poured through her as he stroked a hand through her hair. "Oh, Cooper, that is so wonderful to hear!" She so wanted him to be close to his sister.

"You know what else would be wonderful?" He lifted her hand, kissed the back of it, then held it against his chest over his still racing heart. "If you agreed to marry me," he proposed thickly, his dark eyes serious. And full of all the love she had ever dreamed of. "Not as a means to an end," he continued persuasively, "but for all the right reasons."

Like love and passion and emotional closeness. She met his coaxing smile with one of her own. "I think I can do that."

He kissed her again, promising her tenderly. "We're going to have an incredible future together."

She kissed him back with all the love in her heart. "Yes, Coop," she promised, her hopes for the future growing by leaps and bounds, "we are…"

Epilogue

Two summers later...

Cooper wrapped his arm around Jillian's shoulders and pulled her close. "They're going to love it."

She snuggled against her husband and gazed at the newly installed playset in the backyard. "I think so, too," she murmured.

After all, what was not to love? she thought on a satisfied exhalation.

The wooden set came complete with a play fort, slide, ladder, three swings, a two-person glider, a miniature climbing wall with rope and a fireman's pole to slide down.

Cooper stroked her hand. "Think we're spoiling them?"

Jillian grinned, aware he stole her breath and always would. She nestled closer, inhaling his brisk masculine scent. "Probably." She danced her fingers across the warm solid muscles of his chest. "But we're also providing an outdoor place for them to play with their cousins when they visit."

He bussed the top of her head. "Which is all the time…"

She laughed softly, admitting, "We Lockharts hang together."

Hands sliding to her hips, he turned her to face him. "You do."

Their bodies came together as readily as their lips. Jillian wrapped her arms about his neck and kissed him sweetly. "So it's a good thing you're one of us now."

"Amen to that." His throaty admission led to another soul-stealing kiss.

They drew apart as Jillian's phone signaled an incoming text. She read it. "Mom and Dad want to know if it's okay to bring the kids over to see their birthday surprise before the guests arrive for the party."

"I think that's a really good idea."

Jillian typed in: Absolutely! Thanks! See you soon! She put her phone away. Only to have it ding again. "You're popular today," Cooper teased.

She pulled her cell phone back out. Warmed inside at what she saw. "Desiree is on her way, too. She should be here in fifteen minutes or so."

Cooper's face lit with affection that signaled just how far they had all come. "That's good, too." He paused, his fingers tightening on hers. "I'm really happy she agreed to be a part of all our lives."

Jillian sighed her contentment. "Me, too."

The triplets would know the truth one day, when they were adults and able to handle it. For now, Desiree was their country superstar aunt, who appeared in videos and sang some of their favorite songs on the radio. And occasionally visited.

"It's all worked out better than I ever could have imagined," Jillian reflected.

After a six-month engagement, during which they had shared guardianship, and living space, they had married in a small private ceremony, and formally adopted the triplets. He had finished out the Rock Creek ranch house, and rented it to a young couple who helped him out part-time on the ranch in exchange for a reduced rent.

Jillian had hired two part-time botanists to assist her, too. They were local grad students who had flexible schedules. Which was good, because her antique rose business had been booming since her Old Blush roses had been planted in the Texas governor's mansion flower garden.

"I agree, life is good," Cooper returned fondly.

Jillian petted King, who had come up to stand beside them. "Now all we have to do is figure out how to expand our house to accommodate three growing girls."

He ran a hand across her tummy. "And our baby on the way…"

Jillian smiled as they walked around to the front of the house where the *Happy Birthday Sadie, Tess and Hallie!* banner, several tables worth of goodies and party favors, and a whole host of balloons adorned the front porch. "Think it will be a boy?"

Cooper's eyes twinkled. "Or a girl. Doesn't matter. We will love our new little one just the same."

That they would.

"And we'll hire a builder to add the extra space we need. And make sure it's all done in time…"

Two vehicles turned into the lane. The first belonged to Carol and Robert Lockhart. The second was Desiree's fancy fire-engine-red pickup.

Jillian grinned. "They're here!"

Two minutes later everyone was emerging from their cars.

"Mommy Mommy Mommy! Daddy Daddy Daddy!" the girls chimed as they ran toward them.

Cooper and Jillian gathered them close for a family hug. Carol, Robert and Desiree took up the rear.

They all joined in the group embrace, then watched as the girls raced up onto the porch to check out the party gear. "Can we wear our princess birthday hats now?" Sadie begged.

"I want a balloon," Hallie said.

"And some lemonade, please!" Tess declared.

All requests were met. Then the eight of them went around back to see the newly installed present.

The girls' jaws dropped in awe. "Wow," Tess said.

"For us?" Sadie asked.

"And all your cousins and friends," Cooper affirmed.

"This is awesome!" Hallie jumped up and down, clapping her hands.

"Thank you, Mommy and Daddy!" the girls called one after another as they raced to try out the slide. "This is the best birthday ever!" Sadie declared.

"Best *family* ever," Cooper murmured in Jillian's ear.

Contentment flowing through her, she kissed his jaw, knowing all their dreams had come true.

Her heart swelling with love, she gazed deep into his eyes. The silence communicated everything they had been blessed with. All they felt. "I couldn't agree more," she said.

* * * * *

Watch for the next book in Cathy Gillen Thacker's Lockharts Lost & Found miniseries, which features Navy SEAL Zach Callahan and Faith Lockhart and her soon-to-be adopted infant son, Quinn! Coming December 2021, only from Harlequin Special Edition.

**WE HOPE YOU ENJOYED
THIS BOOK FROM**

**◈ HARLEQUIN
SPECIAL
EDITION**

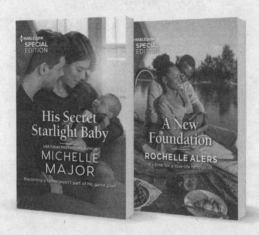

Believe in love. Overcome obstacles. Find happiness.

Relate to finding comfort and strength in the
support of loved ones and enjoy the journey
no matter what life throws your way.

6 NEW BOOKS AVAILABLE EVERY MONTH!

HSEHALO2021

*Uplifting or passionate,
heartfelt or thrilling—
Harlequin has your
happily-ever-after.*

With a wide range of romance series that each
offer new books every month, you are sure to
find the satisfying escape you deserve.

**Look for all Harlequin series
new releases on the
last Tuesday of each month
in stores and online!**

Harlequin.com

HONSALE0521

COMING NEXT MONTH FROM

⊕ HARLEQUIN
SPECIAL EDITION

#2857 THE MOST ELIGIBLE COWBOY
Montana Mavericks: The Real Cowboys of Bronco Heights
by Melissa Senate

Brandon Taylor has zero interest in tying the knot—until his unexpected fling with ex-girlfriend Cassidy Ware. Now she's pregnant—but Cassidy is not jumping at his practical proposal. She remembers their high school romance all too well, and she won't wed without proof that Brandon 2.0 can be the *real* husband she longs for.

#2858 THE LATE BLOOMER'S ROAD TO LOVE
Matchmaking Mamas • by Marie Ferrarella

When other girls her age were dating and finding love, Rachel Fenelli was keeping the family restaurant going after her father's heart attack. Now she's on the verge of starting the life she should have started years ago. Enter Wyatt Watson, the only physical therapist her stubborn dad will tolerate. But little does Rachel know that her dad has an ulterior—matchmaking?—motive.

#2859 THE PUPPY PROBLEM
Paradise Pets • by Katie Meyer

There's nothing single mom Megan Palmer wouldn't do to help her son, Owen. So when his school tries to keep his autism service dog out of the classroom, Megan goes straight to the principal's office—and meets Luke Wright. He's impressed by her, and the more they work together, the more he hopes to win her over...

#2860 A DELICIOUS DILEMMA
by Sera Taíno

Val Navarro knew she shouldn't go dancing right after a bad breakup and she definitely shouldn't be thinking the handsome, sensitive stranger she meets could be more than a rebound. Especially after she finds out his father's company could shut down her Puerto Rican restaurant and unravel her tight-knit neighborhood. Is following her heart a recipe for disaster?

#2861 LAST-CHANCE MARRIAGE RESCUE
Top Dog Dude Ranch • by Catherine Mann

Nina and Douglas Archer are on the verge of divorce, but they're both determined to keep it together for one last family vacation, planned by their ten-year-old twins. And when they do, they're surprised to find themselves giving in to the romance of it all. Still, Nina knows she needs an emotionally available husband. Will a once-in-a-lifetime trip show them the way back to each other?

#2862 THE FAMILY SHE DIDN'T EXPECT
The Culhanes of Cedar River • by Helen Lacey

Marnie Jackson has one mission: to discover her roots in Cedar River. She's determined to fulfill her mother's dying wish, but her sexy landlord and his charming daughters turn out to be a surprising distraction from her goal. Widower Joss Culhane has been focusing on work, his kids and his own family drama. Why risk opening his heart to another woman who might leave them?

**YOU CAN FIND MORE INFORMATION ON UPCOMING HARLEQUIN TITLES,
FREE EXCERPTS AND MORE AT HARLEQUIN.COM.**

HSECNM0821

SPECIAL EXCERPT FROM

⊕HARLEQUIN
SPECIAL EDITION

*When Val Navarro meets Philip Wagner, she believes
she's met the man of her dreams, until she discovers
that his father's company is responsible for the
changes that could shut down her Puerto Rican
restaurant and unravel her tight-knit neighborhood.
When Philip takes over negotiations, Val wants to
believe he has good intentions. But is following her
heart a recipe for disaster?*

*Read on for a sneak peek at
A Delicious Dilemma
by Sera Taíno!*

She returned with the pot of melted chocolate and poured the now-cooled liquid into a cup, handing it to him. Val fussing over him made him feel positively giddy. He raised the cup and took a sip. Chocolate and nutmeg melted on his tongue, sending a surge of pleasure through him.

"Puerto Rican hot chocolate," she said, taking her seat again. "Maybe the sugar will perk you up."

"You're worried about me falling asleep at the wheel."

"This is how I'm made. I'm a worrier."

His eyes flickered to her strong hands, admiring the signs of use, and he wondered at what other things she created with them. "No one's worried about me in a very long time."

He was learning to read her, so he was ready for her zinger. "In my family, worrying is an Olympic sport, so if you ever need someone to worry about you, feel free to borrow any of us."

He smiled into his cup. "I appreciate the offer."

She settled onto the stool, shuffling her feet into and out of her Crocs. "I wasn't really looking for anything tonight."

"Neither was I. But here we are."

Her eyes flicked away again, a habit he was beginning to understand was a nervous reaction, as if she might find the answer to her confusion somewhere in her environment. "That breakup I told you about? That was the last time I've been with anyone."

"Same. It's been a while for me, too." Maybe too long, if his complete lack of confidence right now was any indication.

"Just managing expectations." She poked at her cake, swirling the fork in the fragrant cream. "I'm really not up for anything serious."

"That's fair."

She took a bite, chewing slowly, the gears of her mind visibly working. He didn't rush her, and his patience was rewarded when, after a full minute, she said, "Okay. Next Saturday. I don't work Sundays."

"What if I can't wait until next Saturday?"

"It's like that?" she whispered.

"It's like that," he answered, and she was suddenly so close that if he leaned forward, it would be impossibly easy to kiss her. And he wanted to kiss her badly; the wanting burned hot in his chest. But he couldn't. It would be a lie.

Don't miss
A Delicious Dilemma *by Sera Taíno,*
available September 2021 wherever
Harlequin Special Edition books and ebooks are sold.

Harlequin.com

Copyright © 2021 by Sera Taíno

HSEEXP0821R

Get 4 FREE REWARDS!

We'll send you 2 FREE Books plus 2 FREE Mystery Gifts.

Harlequin Special Edition books relate to finding comfort and strength in the support of loved ones and enjoying the journey no matter what life throws your way.

FREE
Value Over
$20

YES! Please send me 2 FREE Harlequin Special Edition novels and my 2 FREE gifts (gifts are worth about $10 retail). After receiving them, if I don't wish to receive any more books, I can return the shipping statement marked "cancel." If I don't cancel, I will receive 6 brand-new novels every month and be billed just $4.99 per book in the U.S. or $5.74 per book in Canada. That's a savings of at least 12% off the cover price! It's quite a bargain! Shipping and handling is just 50¢ per book in the U.S. and $1.25 per book in Canada.* I understand that accepting the 2 free books and gifts places me under no obligation to buy anything. I can always return a shipment and cancel at any time. The free books and gifts are mine to keep no matter what I decide.

235/335 HDN GNMP

Name (please print)

Address   Apt. #

City   State/Province   Zip/Postal Code

Email: Please check this box ☐ if you would like to receive newsletters and promotional emails from Harlequin Enterprises ULC and its affiliates. You can unsubscribe anytime.

Mail to the **Harlequin Reader Service:**
IN U.S.A.: P.O. Box 1341, Buffalo, NY 14240-8531
IN CANADA: P.O. Box 603, Fort Erie, Ontario L2A 5X3

Want to try 2 free books from another series! Call 1-800-873-8635 or visit www.ReaderService.com.

*Terms and prices subject to change without notice. Prices do not include sales taxes, which will be charged (if applicable) based on your state or country of residence. Canadian residents will be charged applicable taxes. Offer not valid in Quebec. This offer is limited to one order per household. Books received may not be as shown. Not valid for current subscribers to Harlequin Special Edition books. All orders subject to approval. Credit or debit balances in a customer's account(s) may be offset by any other outstanding balance owed by or to the customer. Please allow 4 to 6 weeks for delivery. Offer available while quantities last.

Your Privacy—Your information is being collected by Harlequin Enterprises ULC, operating as Harlequin Reader Service. For a complete summary of the information we collect, how we use this information and to whom it is disclosed, please visit our privacy notice located at corporate.harlequin.com/privacy-notice. From time to time we may also exchange your personal information with reputable third parties. If you wish to opt out of this sharing of your personal information, please visit readerservice.com/consumerschoice or call 1-800-873-8635. **Notice to California Residents**—Under California law, you have specific rights to control and access your data. For more information on these rights and how to exercise them, visit corporate.harlequin.com/california-privacy.

HSE21R

Don't miss the fourth book in the touching and romantic Rendezvous Falls series from

JO McNALLY

It's never too late for a second chance...

"Sure to please readers of contemporary romance."
—*New York Journal of Books* on *Barefoot on a Starlit Night*

Order your copy today!

HQNBooks.com

PHJMBPA0721R

Love Harlequin romance?

DISCOVER.

Be the first to find out about promotions, news and exclusive content!

f Facebook.com/HarlequinBooks

🐦 Twitter.com/HarlequinBooks

📷 Instagram.com/HarlequinBooks

📌 Pinterest.com/HarlequinBooks

You Tube YouTube.com/HarlequinBooks

ReaderService.com

EXPLORE.

Sign up for the Harlequin e-newsletter and download a free book from any series at **TryHarlequin.com**

CONNECT.

Join our Harlequin community to share your thoughts and connect with other romance readers!
Facebook.com/groups/HarlequinConnection

HARLEQUIN

HSOCIAL2021